KU-450-772

'I thought we'd already decided I wasn't a gentleman.' Cameron's amused smile held a touch of wickedness. 'My room is this way, too. 427.'

Ginger flushed, feeling foolish. 'Of course. Sorry. 428.'

Her breath felt ridiculously shallow, which had nothing to do with having used the stairs. She couldn't explain how she was feeling. They hesitated outside their doors, entry cards in hand. She knew she should just say goodnight and turn away, but there was something so mesmerising about him, and something weird was going on between them. Everything about him—his mouth, his eyes, his humour, his air of danger— captivated her.

Later, she could never have said who moved first. One second there was a safe gap of three feet between them, the next she was in his arms, her own wrapped around his neck, exchanging the most mind-blowing, nerve-tingling, exhilarating kiss of her entire life.

Dear Reader

One special night could change their lives for ever...

I am very excited to welcome you to my fourth Medical™ Romance and to Strathlochan! This fictional town gives me the opportunity to broaden the scope while maintaining the rural Scottish flavour of my stories. I'm looking forward to introducing you to new characters whose lives intertwine with some old favourites, building a whole new interconnected community—one I hope you will come to know and love as much as I am enjoying creating it.

We start this new series with ONE SPECIAL NIGHT…, the story of Cameron and Ginger, two dedicated, caring doctors whose pasts have led them to choose their individual specialties and who devote themselves to their patients to the exclusion of all else. I hope you enjoy the ups and downs as Cameron and Ginger battle the conflict that threatens to keep them apart; the push-pull as they each fight for the ongoing survival of their clinics while resisting what seems an impossible attraction…sparked by one special night. Can they find a way to balance their professional and personal lives? Or will love and happiness be sacrificed as they put the needs of their patients before their need for each other?

If you enjoy this introduction to Strathlochan, please come back and meet the next couple, Frazer and Callie. Look out for their story in the Mills & Boon® Christmas anthology. I'll look forward to seeing you then!

Happy reading

Margaret

ONE SPECIAL NIGHT...

BY
MARGARET McDONAGH

MILLS & BOON
Pure reading pleasure

All the characters in this book have no existence outside the imagination of the author, and have no relation whatsoever to anyone bearing the same name or names. They are not even distantly inspired by any individual known or unknown to the author, and all the incidents are pure invention.

All Rights Reserved including the right of reproduction in whole or in part in any form. This edition is published by arrangement with Harlequin Enterprises II BV/S.à.r.l. The text of this publication or any part thereof may not be reproduced or transmitted in any form or by any means, electronic or mechanical, including photocopying, recording, storage in an information retrieval system, or otherwise, without the written permission of the publisher.

® and TM are trademarks owned and used by the trademark owner and/or its licensee. Trademarks marked with ® are registered with the United Kingdom Patent Office and/or the Office for Harmonisation in the Internal Market and in other countries.

First published in Great Britain 2007
Large Print edition 2008
Harlequin Mills & Boon Limited,
Eton House, 18-24 Paradise Road,
Richmond, Surrey TW9 1SR

MANCHESTER
PUBLIC
LIBRARIES

© Margaret McDonagh 2007

ISBN: 978 0 263 19935 2

Set in Times Roman 16½ on 19 pt.
17-0208-54373

Printed and bound in Great Britain
by Antony Rowe Ltd, Chippenham, Wiltshire

Margaret McDonagh says of herself: 'I began losing myself in the magical world of books from a very young age, and I always knew that I had to write—pursuing the dream for over twenty years, often with cussed stubbornness in the face of rejection letters! Despite having numerous romance novellas, short stories and serials published, the news that my first "proper book" had been accepted by Harlequin Mills & Boon for their Medical™ Romance line brought indescribable joy! Having a passion for learning makes researching an involving pleasure, and I love developing new characters, getting to know them, setting them challenges to overcome. The hardest part is saying goodbye to them, because they become so real to me. And I always fall in love with my heroes! Writing and reading books, keeping in touch with friends, watching sport and meeting the demands of my four-legged companions keeps me well occupied. I hope you enjoy reading this book as much as I loved writing it.'

http://margaretmcdonagh.bravehost.com
margaret.mcdonagh@hotmail.co.uk

Recent titles by the same author:

HIS VERY SPECIAL NURSE
A DOCTOR WORTH WAITING FOR
THE ITALIAN DOCTOR'S BRIDE

To the usual suspects,
for all their friendship and support

To Liz Fielding, Kate Hardy,
Anne McAllister and Kate Walker,
for their kindness and generosity, and for
providing such marvellous inspiration

And to all at the Pink Heart Society—
Trish, Nic, Ally and Natasha,
for getting it up and running—
and all the writers and readers supporting
the wonderful world of romance fiction
www.pinkheartsociety.blogspot.com

CHAPTER ONE

DR GINGER O'NEILL noticed the man the moment he stepped onto the train. It was hard to miss him. Six feet tall and athletically built, he commanded attention. Especially female attention. His short dark hair was shot through with a few threads of steel grey at the temples, giving him a distinguished, compelling appeal, and she judged him to be in his mid-thirties, a few years older than herself. Dressed in worn, snug-fitting jeans and a black T-shirt, whose cut-off sleeves displayed tanned, leanly muscled arms, he looked cool despite the August heat wave.

Given the way her heart had begun thudding erratically under her ribs at one sight of his roguish good looks, he ought to carry a government health warning. Which was ridiculous because she was always cool, rational and practical, and never swayed by a pretty face. Not that he was *pretty*. More… divinely, scrumptiously gorgeous. But the principle should apply.

Ginger cursed herself, unable to stop watching the man as he walked down the carriage towards her. His features were the kind a sculptor dreamed of modelling—a determined jaw, currently shadowed with a day's growth of stubble, a straight nose, lean cheeks and the sexiest, most irresistibly sinful mouth she had ever seen, his full lower lip swelling under a finely shaped top one. Her gaze roved upwards, encountering speculative grey eyes fringed with long, thick lashes.

Discomfited, Ginger managed to drag her disobedient gaze away and busied herself settling into her place behind a table, arranging her notes and laptop. Her pulse raced, her awareness increasing, as the man selected the table across the aisle from her. As he reached up to stow a bag in the overhead locker, his T-shirt rode up to expose a strip of tanned, muscled back above the low-slung waistband of jeans that lovingly moulded his impressive rear end. Strangely breathless, she could almost feel her tongue hanging out as she stared at him.

Horrified at her reaction, she turned away, conscious of him sliding gracefully along the seat and sorting out his own papers. With a half empty carriage, why did he have to sit right there so every time she raised her head she couldn't help but see him?

As the train pulled out of Strathlochan station, beginning the long journey from Scotland to London, Ginger endeavoured to read through the presentation she was to give at her meeting the next afternoon. It would be the most important hour of her life. She had to make the best effort possible if she was to secure the money she needed to develop her own eating disorders clinic, one which would provide desperately needed residential places as well as a day centre and outpatient facilities.

Nervous at the daunting prospect ahead of her, she recalled the discussion she had shared with Pip Beaumont, friend, right-hand woman and the best mental health nurse she had ever known…

'Ginger! I thought you were supposed to have left a couple of hours ago,' Pip had exclaimed, waylaying her as she'd hurried towards the main doors of the hospital.

'You and me both. I was held up with morning appointments—one of which was with Danielle Watson. She's lost another couple of kilos and I'm troubled about her emotional state. She's being bullied at school again. If you have time while I'm away, would you review her latest diary pages and see if you have some ideas? I left them in her file.'

A worried frown had creased Pip's brow. 'Yes, of course I will.'

'Are you due to see her?'

'Not before your appointment with her next week.' Pip had paused a moment. 'But I'll fit her in for a chat in the next couple of days. Somehow.'

'Thanks. I know how crammed the schedule is, but I think that would be a good idea.'

'You're worried she's bordering on depression again?'

Ginger grimaced, concerned for the teenager who, having lost her parents three years ago, had little support at home, living as she did with a cousin who seemed uninterested in the girl's care. 'There's a risk of it. And if she keeps losing weight, she's going to endanger herself. I really want to turn things round and avoid having to admit her if at all possible.'

'I'll take care of it. What else is worrying you?' her friend asked with customary insight, and Ginger sighed, pausing outside the door.

'I was heading out of the office when I received an untimely summons to see the powers that be.' She juggled her overnight bag, laptop and sundry items as she tried to glance at her watch, thankful that her personal assistant, Sarah, had checked train times and rebooked her ticket. 'I'm leaving for the station now.'

'I'll give you a lift.'

A relieved smile curved Ginger's mouth. 'Are you sure? That would be great.'

'It will save you time if you don't have to worry about your car.'

'Thanks, Pip.'

'So, what was the summons about?' Pip asked once they were crammed into her tiny, purple Fiat and heading out of Strathlochan hospital's car park.

As they travelled down the hill, the town spread across the wooded valley and around the edge of a small loch, Ginger's mood darkened. With a sigh, she recalled her earlier audience with her department head and one member of the hospital management board. Usually slow to anger, the one thing guaranteed to stir her temper was anything that adversely affected her patients, and what she had heard a short while ago had been the worst possible news.

'You don't want to know.'

'That bad?' Worry was evident in Pip's usually cheerful voice. 'Tell me, lovey.'

'Not only have my pleas for increased funding been turned down but department changes and cost-cutting mean the unit will be disbanded next spring and reabsorbed into the general psychological services.'

'Oh, no! That's even worse than we anticipated. Ginger, they can't!'

Upset, she ran the fingers of one hand through her flyaway hair. 'Unfortunately they can…and they will.' Damn them, she cursed silently, tension tightening her every nerve and sinew.

'Then tomorrow's appointment is even more imperative.'

Pip's quiet words echoed Ginger's own sentiments. 'Exactly.'

'What time is the meeting?'

'Not until two. I'm only leaving now because I want to be fresh for the presentation, and they paid for my travel and accommodation.' Ginger sucked in a breath as she considered the enormity of the next twenty-four hours. 'Oh, Pip, I just hope I can pull this off. I *have* to.'

Her friend reached out and patted her arm. 'If anyone can, it's you.'

'Thanks.' Ginger managed a smile, warmed by the loyalty and reassurance.

Pip halted at a road junction, her mousy curls swinging across her shoulders as she shook her head. 'I can't believe we're going to be closed down. Whatever do management think our patients are going to do without the unit? They need specialist care. With the best will in the world, an overstretched general department can't give that. The lucky ones have parents who can afford private treatment, but that doesn't help the majority, does it?'

'No, it doesn't. Not to mention how far they'll have to travel to find another dedicated eating disorders centre. Goodness knows, there are few enough of them in the UK.' Ginger clenched her hands together, weighed down by her sense of responsibility and concern for the young people in her care. 'I have to get my own clinic open, Pip. Somehow we have to find the money.'

In the months since the rumour of possible department changes and cost-cutting had first shocked her team, and sparked the idea to branch out on her own, she had worked hard on a business plan. Discussions with the health trust had elicited a provisional agreement that, if the hospital unit downgraded and Ginger's project took off, they would outsource services to her for those NHS patients who needed specialist referral. She had a core number of staff keen to join her, support from regional GPs, and she even had the promise of money from a few sources... grateful parents, charitable organisations, a bank loan and, tentatively, the NHS referral funding. Which still left an enormous hole in a financial budget that was frighteningly high. The start-up expenses alone were horrendous, without the annual running costs. But she would find a way. She had to. She couldn't, *wouldn't,* let her patients down.

'An unexpected benefactor seems too good to be true.' Pip's comment drew her from her thoughts. 'Who is Sir Morrison Ackerman, do you know?'

Ginger shook her head. 'He was described to me as Britain's cross between Paul Getty, Bill Gates and Donald Trump!'

'If he's as rich and generous, we'll all be happy.' Hazel eyes twinkled as Pip glanced at her with a smile. 'Why is he doing this?'

'All I know is that he was born locally, but now lives in America where he made his substantial fortune. He's given a lot of money to global aid charities and now he wants to put something back into his old community.' Ginger paused as she recalled the brief details she had been given. 'Apparently he has a special interest in the work we do, something about a problem in the family years ago. That's why we are on a shortlist of three for this donation and sponsorship.'

'Are you actually going to meet him?'

'I imagine so. With his lawyers and business advisors. I was told he was stopping over in London for a day *en route* from America to his holiday villa in Italy. The three of us called to represent our various projects each have one hour to make our presentation and explain why we deserve to get his money.'

Pip gave a little shiver as she pulled the car in outside the station. 'Scary.'

'You can say that again!' Ginger felt a renewed attack of nerves. 'It would make all the difference to getting the clinic off the ground. And I'm determined to win. Even if I really can't afford to lose the two days this trip is taking me away from my patients.'

'We'll cope. And it will be worth it in the long run if the funding is forthcoming. Besides, you work far too hard, Ginger, so try and enjoy it as a break. Have a bit of an adventure,' Pip advised with a smile.

Ginger's answering smile was wry. 'I don't think there will be much time for fun on this trip.'

'Who are the other two in the running for the money?'

'I don't know.' Ginger struggled to get herself and her things out of Pip's too-small car. 'They're keeping everything very hush-hush at the moment. I'm not supposed to talk to anyone else about it.'

Pip's eyebrows rose, and she tapped her nose with one finger, her expression conspiratorial. 'Mum's the word!'

her sitting behind the table, she was wearing a floaty skirt with a predominance of the colour lavender in it, and a cream short-sleeved top that, while not being obvious, failed to mask her delicious, womanly curves. She could be anywhere from twenty upwards, he thought, although she had the bearing and self-assurance of a woman nearer thirty.

Annoyed with himself, he snapped his laptop shut and took out the papers whose delayed arrival had made him late leaving home and had caused him to miss the earlier train he had been booked on. His friend, Iain Chamberlain, had seen his car in the drive, and had stopped at the cottage on his way down the lane as he'd headed back to his office after lunch…

'I thought you were going to London.'

Leaving Iain to close the front door and trail in his wake, Cameron had scowled with impatience, pacing back to his study. 'I was. I am. Some papers haven't arrived and I can't leave without them. I'm waiting for them to be faxed through now.'

'Bummer.' Amusement had laced his friend's voice.

An answering smile had pulled at Cameron's mouth. 'Exactly.'

'And here I was thinking your return to Strathlochan was meant to deliver you a less hassled lifestyle!'

'Yeah? Where did you get that crazy idea from?' Despite his edgy mood, Cameron had laughed. 'I've been working harder than ever, knocking things into shape. Everything depends on the outcome of tomorrow's meeting. If that comes off, things will be so hectic here I may have to go back to London for a rest!'

Iain's brown eyes had darkened with rueful amusement. 'Sure. Like you're not the most driven, work-obsessed guy I know! Fancy a lift to the station?'

'Are you sure? That would save time—if the papers ever come, that is. I thought it was too good to be true that everything fitted neatly together for a simple three-day trip.'

'When do you start your hospital work?'

His impatience growing, Cameron checked his watch again. 'First Monday of September. I'll be doing some part-time consultations until my own project gets going. Plus the private patients and self-help groups I already have up and running. I—' He broke off as the fax machine clattered to life. 'About bloody time.'

They probably broke the odd speed limit heading into Strathlochan so he could catch the next London-bound train, Cameron admitted, but nothing and no one was going to stand in the way of him achieving his ends. The new self-harm facility he planned for the area was far too important, not just to him but to the patients who depended on him. Iain had accused him of being driven. He was. He had to be. Pain threatened to swamp him with unbearable memories. Once he had been too late, had let someone down. He was going to do everything in his power to make sure that *never* happened again.

Iain pulled up in front of the station, taking the place of a ridiculous-looking purple Fiat that drew away ahead of them. 'Good luck.'

'Thanks, Iain.' Cameron ruthlessly banished his dark thoughts, grabbed his things and closed the door, leaning in the window for a parting goodbye. 'I'll see you and Maxine when I get back. Take care of my godchild—I don't want him born before I get back.'

'Maxine's reply to that would burn your ears! She wants junior out of there right now. She says she's never letting me near her again.'

Curbing a rush of bitter memories, Cameron managed a smile. 'I don't blame her!'

Now, lulled by the rhythm of the train, Cameron leaned back against the seat and contemplated this dual-purpose trip to London. It was going to be hectic, and he would rather not have been called as an expert witness for a court case on the same day he had to present his proposals for his own project. But he had promised, and the sooner it was over the sooner he could leave London for good and devote all his energies to his future plans in Strathlochan.

Movement diverted his attention and he sneaked a sideways glance in time to see the woman push her notepad aside. With an audible sigh of frustration she set down her pen. Closing her eyes, she gathered up her long hair, tilting her head back to let whatever breeze the tiny window delivered fan across her neck and throat. The actions caused her top to tighten over the lushest of breasts. Cameron swallowed as raw, animal desire stabbed through him. No wonder the poor guy who had briefly sat opposite her had tried so ineptly to chat her up. If she did this hair-and-arched-neck thing again, he wouldn't be responsible for his own actions.

That she was innocently unaware of her desirability, and completely without artifice, was apparent when she released her hair, allowing it to fall like a golden halo round her face and shoulders. She glanced round, smothering a yawn, her iridescent turquoise eyes widening in shock as she met his gaze. Cameron did nothing to hide his masculine appreciation, seeing a flush of awareness wash across her cheeks before she folded her arms across her delightful chest and hurriedly looked back at her work.

What was the matter with him? He was heading to London on one of the most important missions of his life, and all he could do was fantasise over a stranger's breasts! His gaze strayed once more. Damn, but she was one sexy woman. He shifted uncomfortably as his body responded in the most basic of ways. This was ridiculous! The randy teenage years were decades behind him. He was a thirty-six-year-old consultant, not a schoolboy. And he didn't do relationships, didn't get involved, not any more. In his years in London, the 'after Lisa years', he'd had occasional evenings out with sophisticated, independent women who had wanted nothing more from their brief association than he had. Which had suited him fine. But more and more, all his energies were going into his work. Nothing could be allowed to distract him from his goal. He'd do well to remember that and stop leching over his unwitting travelling companion.

Ginger felt light-headed and peculiarly breathless. The way he'd just looked at her was outrageous! She was fifteen years past the blushing virgin stage, but she didn't think any man had ever regarded at her so...so...*sexually* before. Heat flared inside her, making her ache with an electrifying desire and, even more shockingly, it wasn't abating. This was ridiculous!

She forced herself to think of mundane things and looked out of the window at the changing landscape, the rural scenery giving way to urban environments as the train sped south. Her preference when travelling by train had always been to sit 'facing the engine', as her father would once have put it. Perhaps it said something about her, that she needed to see where she was going, to approach things head on. Her wickedly attractive travelling companion, on the other hand, whose reflection she could see in the glass, looked perfectly relaxed with his back to the way they were going. Did that mean he was someone who dwelt too much on the past? It was an odd thought, but an occupational hazard, she supposed, to look for the analytical reasons behind people's behaviour.

When her mobile phone sounded, the personalised ring tone seeming louder than usual, Ginger fumbled in her bag to answer it, far too aware of the man nearby, her cheeks warming again as she met an amused grey gaze.

'Sorry.' She saw him shake his head at her apology before she turned aside to take the call, seeing her assistant's name on the display. 'Yes, Sarah?'

'I'm sorry, Ginger, but I've had Mr Carstairs on the phone. He's the father of the new girl you will be seeing on Monday.'

'Yes, I know.' Ginger frowned, recalling the brief case details she had received from the GP who had referred Tess Carstairs to her. 'What's the problem?'

'He says he's not sure about the appointment, whether coming to the clinic is in the best interests of his daughter,' Sarah informed her, anxiety in her voice.

'I see. I'd be interested to know how he thinks they're going to change things themselves.' She curbed her frustration and annoyance. Eating disorders carried an unfair stigma, and this was not the first time she had dealt with parents who were more worried about what other people might think rather than their child's troubles. Dr Nic di Angelis, the family GP, had already warned her of the father's attitude in this case. 'Has Mr Carstairs cancelled the appointment?'

'No, but he wants to talk more about it with you first. I explained you were away for a couple of days. He got a bit shirty.'

Ginger was alerted by the thread of upset Sarah was unable to hide. 'Shirty? How?'

'He swore at me, actually, when I wouldn't give him your mobile number.'

'Did he indeed?' She paused, finding a blank

page to make a note in her diary. 'I'm sorry you had to put up with that, Sarah. I'll deal with it.'

'Do you want me to give you his number?'

Knowing she would have scant privacy to discuss confidential matters on the train, Ginger declined. 'Not now. There's little I can do from here. If he rings again, say you have informed me and I'll telephone him on Friday when I'm back in the office. All right?'

'Yes, fine.'

'And such rudeness is unacceptable, Sarah. If he speaks to you like that again, you have my permission to hang up. Tell Pip and Andrew what I have said, and if there is any further trouble with him while I'm gone, refer him to them.'

'OK.' Sarah's relief was obvious. 'Thanks, Ginger.'

'No problem. Anything else while we're on?'

'Nothing important. I'm really sorry for bothering you.'

'You haven't bothered me.' Ginger smiled, knowing how efficient but sensitive the twenty-one-year-old was. 'It's not your fault, Sarah. You get off home on time and don't worry about it.'

'I will. Good luck, again.'

After hanging up, Ginger made a few more notes, very cross at the behaviour of Tess Carstairs's father, and concerned for the girl's well-being. She would review her notes carefully before talking to the parents. Whether Mr Carstairs wanted to believe it or not, his daughter needed help, and Ginger was determined to do all she could to make sure Tess received it.

Concerned that her phone call had disturbed the man nearby, she glanced across, plucking up the nerve to speak to him. Before she could decide whether to say anything or leave it be, he seemed to sense her regard, turning to meet her gaze. Ginger swallowed, feeling the pull of attraction across the narrow distance that separated them.

'I just wanted to apologise about the phone,' she explained, sounding uncharacteristically husky.

'No problem.' His voice, deep and throaty, sent a shiver down her spine. 'One of the hazards of twenty-first-century living.'

'Yes.'

As if to illustrate the point, his own phone chose that moment to beep with an incoming text message. He raised an eyebrow at the irony, and Ginger was aware of an intense moment of shared amusement and connection before he turned away to read his text, frowning as he tapped a hasty reply, then returned his attention to his work.

Thirsty and unsettled, and still with a long way to go, she took her bag, laptop and confidential papers, before manoeuvring out from behind the table to head for the on-train shop. Having missed lunch, she chose a chilled smoothie to drink, and selected an apple, before making her way back to the carriage. As she approached her seat, the train jolted, and she gave a cry of surprise as she missed her footing. Instantly, a hand was there to steady her. Firm and protective, masculine fingers closed on the bare skin of her arm, sending what felt like several million volts zinging through every nerve-ending in her body. She gasped in shock, unable to prevent herself looking at him, the answering awareness in his grey eyes blatant.

Realising his fingers were still holding her, setting every atom of her being thrumming with sensation, Ginger moved away, breaking the un-settling contact. 'Thanks.' She hastened back behind her table with a distinct lack of elegance.

'No problem,' the man repeated, a frown on his face.

Conscious of the prickle of desire that continued to pulse through her, Ginger sipped her tangy cranberry and raspberry smoothie, and tried to refocus her attention on her presentation. Reaching for her apple, she felt the man's gaze on her but she studiously tried to ignore him. She took a bite of the crisp, juicy fruit, wishing the train would hurry up and speed her to London.

Cameron's frown deepened. He'd lost all concentration and motivation. First he had found himself listening to the woman's smoky voice when she'd taken her call, hearing her annoyance at whatever news had been imparted, but impressed with her handling of what he presumed was a disgruntled secretary. Then her husky apology to him, followed by the sympathetic and amused smile when his text had arrived, had tightened his stomach—and other notable places. He'd sucked in a breath when she'd stood up to get a drink, finding her taller and even more deliciously curvaceous than he had anticipated, but the charge of electricity that had shot through him like a lightning bolt when he had instinctively reached out to steady her had really unnerved him. From the look on her face she had felt the connection, too. And now he was meant to sit here while she ate that apple? He gritted his teeth, watching as her pink tongue tip peeped out to wipe away the succulent juice glistening on her lips, experiencing a raging desire to taste her. Hell! The sooner he got off this train the better!

CHAPTER TWO

THE skies opened as the train approached London, the build-up of atmospheric pressure resulting in a spectacular thunderstorm, with lightning streaking over the capital's rooftops, ominous black clouds darkening the early evening sky. The static electricity that seemed to be crackling across the aisle between her and the man, however, continued to sizzle. Thankful to have arrived, Ginger struggled to gather her belongings, and lost no time escaping the carriage while he was still engaged in extracting his bag from the overhead locker. Hastening down the platform, Ginger crossed the concourse towards the exit and searched for a taxi.

There weren't any.

'Damn it!'

This was all she needed. She still felt on edge

after the unnerving encounter on the train, and removing herself from the man's disturbing presence had done little to minimise the effect he'd had on her. She felt a flicker of regret that she would never see him again, but all her focus had to be on her patients and her responsibility to them, her need to make this trip a success.

'Just do what you've come here to do and get home,' she instructed herself, cursing her lack of protective covering as the rain continued unabated.

Feeling increasingly limp and bedraggled, Ginger walked away from the station, hoping she would have better luck away from the growing queues of people exiting the station. Out on one of the busy side streets, she spotted a vacant taxi and flagged it down, charging for the door and bundling herself inside, nearly banging her head as the opposite door opened and someone else rushed in, threatening to steal her ride.

'Hey!' she complained.

'I don't believe this!'

The throaty growl warned her, and she looked up to encounter a familiar, but unimpressed, steel-grey gaze. 'You!' Oh, help, she thought she had seen the last of him.

'Are you following me?'

The ego of the man! 'Don't flatter yourself. Perhaps you're following me.'

'You've got a nerve. This is my taxi.' Dripping wet hair plastered to his head, he scowled at her with an absence of his previous humour.

'I think you'll find the driver pulled over for me. And I was inside first.' A falsely sweet smile fixed on her face she sat down and closed the door. 'A gentleman would give in gracefully.'

He stared at her, his expression intense, heating her blood and trapping the air in her lungs. 'That's a bit sexist, isn't it? Anyway, what makes you think I'm a gentleman?'

Ginger swallowed. Nothing whatever, if truth be told. She'd decided right off he was more than a tad dangerous and nothing had dispelled that impression. A tense silence stretched between them.

'Are you folks going anywhere or not?' The taxi driver turned to address them, his frustration clear. 'Make up your minds.'

'The City Park Hotel,' they said in unison.

Ginger stared in amazement. 'You're joking?'

'I'm afraid not.' A slow smile played at his sexily pouting mouth. 'Looks like we're sharing and neither of us will have to decide to be gentlemanly—or ladylike—and give in.'

Hearing the taxi driver chuckle, Ginger sat back on the seat and maintained a stony silence, far too aware of the imposing male presence beside her. Fortunately, it was not a long drive, and although the streets were busy, the traffic was moving. She was wet, tired and not a little frazzled from the muggy heat that had sapped everyone's energy for the last three weeks and which the storm appeared to be doing little to dispel.

The next problem arose over paying for the taxi, the driver beaming as they each stuck a high-value note in his hand, determined not to be outdone. Fuming, Ginger carried her things through the front entrance of the small but comfortable hotel, and stalked to the far end of the reception desk, away from her tormentor, to register.

'Just the one night, please.' She smiled at the clerk after giving her name. 'There should be a booking for me.'

'Yes, I have it here. Please, fill in the slip. Would you like some help with your bags?'

'No, I'm fine, thanks.'

Grateful that this was not some large and expensive hotel that would have made her feel out of place, Ginger accepted her key card and turned around, smothering a groan when she saw her nemesis heading for the lifts at the same time as herself. The sooner she was away from him the better, she decided, conscious of the woodsy fragrance of warm male as the lift doors opened and he stepped inside behind her, the small space confining them in far-too-close proximity.

'Which floor?' he asked with resignation.

'Fourth, please.'

A small sigh escaped as he pressed the button on the panel and the doors closed. 'Figures.'

'What does that mean?' Her eyes narrowing, she speared him with a look as the lift began a slow climb upwards.

'Just that it's my floor, too. We seem to be stuck with each other.'

She wished he had chosen a different expression as the words were barely out of his mouth when the lift gave a shudder and ground to a halt, the main light going out, trapping them together in semi-darkness.

'Oh, please. Not this!' Ginger exclaimed.

Her companion swore pithily. She knew just

how he felt. Tamping down her concern, she watched as he pressed the alarm button, then picked up the emergency phone to alert whoever answered that there was a fault.

'They think it's to do with the lightning. Probably a power surge or something.' With another sigh, he hung up the receiver. 'They'll have us out as soon as they can.'

'Thank goodness for that.'

Muttering grimly, she sank down to sit on the floor, drawing her knees up and wrapping her arms around them. In the confined space, and with their assorted belongings, there wasn't a lot of room. A shiver of apprehension rippled through her. Given the exhilarating sports she indulged in during her rare free time, it seemed pathetic to be spooked by this experience, but she was.

'Scared?' He pushed a bag out of the way then sat down across from her, leaning back against the opposite wall.

'Of course not,' she scoffed, then, in the glow from the emergency lights, she noticed the thread of anxiety on his face. 'A bit. You?'

His smile was self-deprecating. 'Being shut in a lift is not my idea of fun.'

'Or mine.' She smiled back, impressed he could admit it and not play the macho tough guy. 'Claustrophobic?'

'Not often but...'

The lift gave a faint judder and they stared at each other in wary silence.

'We need to do something to take our minds off it,' Ginger decided briskly.

'Good idea.' His voice dropped, sounding huskier and more intimate. 'Any suggestions?'

Ginger sucked in a ragged breath. She hoped he wasn't thinking what she was thinking. Not that she should be thinking it herself, but he really was the most devilishly sexy man she'd ever seen! And his mouth was enough to tempt a saint. Forcing herself to banish increasingly erotic thoughts, she shifted uncomfortably and tried to think of something less dangerous.

'My name's Ginger O'Neill, by the way.'

'Cameron Kincaid.'

She was relieved he didn't reach across and offer to shake hands because she didn't think touching him again was a good idea. 'What do you do?'

'For a living?'

'Mmm.'

'What do you think?' he teased, stretching long, denim-clad legs out in front of him.

OK, she could play this game. She paused a moment, regarding him speculatively. 'I think you're a hit man.'

'A hit man?' Laughter rumbled from his chest, the rich sound of it swirling a wave of awareness through her. 'Why a hit man?'

'I don't know. Dark, dangerous, a bit intimidating.'

'Am I?'

He unnerved the hell out of her. 'What about me?'

'You're not intimidating.' Even in the dim light she could see the mischief in his eyes. 'Although the guy on the train who tried to chat you up might have other ideas about that.'

Ginger couldn't help laughing, too. 'I meant, what do you think I do for a living?'

'Undercover spy?'

'Of course not!'

'TV presenter?'

'Nope.'

His gaze assessed her, a look of heated consideration on his face. 'Lingerie model?'

'No way!'

'Pity!'

Warmth flushed her cheeks, embarrassment bringing an edge of chastisement to her voice. 'Cameron.'

Ginger had no illusions about her looks. She would never be a raving beauty, still less a svelte, reed-thin model who looked great in anything. However, she was comfortable with her natural body shape, her curves. And her hectic work schedule, combined with sport when the opportunity allowed, kept her fit and healthy. Daily, she saw the results of far too many tragic attempts to conform to a supposed desirable norm in modern society to ever get dragged down that road herself. Cameron's evident male appreciation made her pulse race, especially when she recalled the frankly sexual way he had looked at her on the train. What she didn't know was what, if anything, to do about it. She couldn't lose sight of her reason for being in London.

Cameron regretted embarrassing Ginger. He would never normally have said anything so provocative, especially to a complete stranger. She probably thought him a complete pervert now, but he seemed to act out of character whenever she was near him. Ginger pushed all his buttons...many of them long forgotten and presumed to no longer be in full working order. He was trying to think of a way to rescue their easy banter when the emergency phone rang and he rose to his feet to answer it, grateful for the reprieve.

'Hello?'

'This is Station Officer Woods from the local fire service. You folks all right? How many of you are there in the lift?'

'Two. We're doing OK.' In the dim light, Cameron sent Ginger a reassuring smile. 'You getting us out of here?'

'As soon as we can. We'd prefer to carefully lower the lift car down, but the mechanism has seized solid, so that isn't going to work this time. You've come to rest about three feet lower than the third floor. Once we're sure the brake is secure and everything is safe, we'll open the doors and bring you out that way. Won't be long now.'

'Thanks.'

Spirits lifted by the news, he relayed the details to Ginger. Sure enough, it wasn't long before there were noises outside and the doors were forced open, flooding them with light. A couple of firefighters grinned down at them.

'How are you doing?'

'We're glad to see you.' Cameron turned to check on Ginger, helping her to her feet.

She swiftly released his hand and stepped away. 'I'm all right.'

'Can you manage, or do you want us to fetch a ladder?' one of the firefighters asked.

'We'll manage.' Ginger's response was immediate, and he imagined she didn't want to linger in here any longer than he did.

Cameron passed their assorted belongings out, and then gestured Ginger forward. 'You go first and I can help you.'

'Thanks.'

Two firefighters took her hands and Cameron gave her a boost, being granted a tantalising flash of luscious creamy thighs and lacy lavender panties. It had a terrible effect on his already wayward libido. Hell! His mind started wondering if her bra matched. He'd love to find out. Love even more to peel it off and... Stop it! Getting himself in check, he vaulted out of the lift, to be greeted by a concerned hotel manager hovering behind the fire crew.

'This is terrible, I cannot apologise enough,' the man gushed obsequiously. 'Please, accept dinner on the house as recompense.'

'That's really not necessary,' Ginger stated.

Cameron nodded his agreement. 'No, it's fine. We're both OK.'

'But I insist! It's the very least the hotel can do.'

So much for their combined protests, Ginger thought with a smile as she was shown to a table in the cosy dining room half an hour later, having showered and changed and restored herself to some semblance of normality. Except that she could still feel the touch of Cameron's hands on her when he had helped her from the lift.

'Your companion will be here directly,' the waiter informed her.

Ginger frowned. 'My what?' Her gaze strayed towards the entrance and she saw that Cameron was being led across to her. 'Excuse me, he's not… I mean, we're not…' Oh, hell!

Dressed in smart dark grey trousers and a matching shirt, the outfit seemed to heighten his dangerous edge and highlight the colour of his eyes and hair. He looked amazing, she admitted, noting too that he hadn't shaved, still having the rakish, piratical air she found so compelling.

'I'm sorry about this.' He smiled as he sat down.

'Don't worry. It seems easier to go with the flow under the circumstances.'

Ginger couldn't help but be affected by the electricity that simmered between them as they studied their menus and placed their orders.

'I'll stick with mineral water, thank you,' she decided, when wine was offered. She definitely needed to keep a clear head around this man.

'Me, too.'

She glanced up, fearing she'd spoken the words out loud. 'Sorry?'

'The mineral water,' Cameron explained.

'Oh!' She sent him a relieved smile. 'Of course.'

Ginger was thankful when their food came and the need to make small talk was removed for a while. The growing tension was undeniable and they had just about exhausted safe topics of conversation, such as the weather. Her meal was delicious, and she realised how hungry she was, having had nothing but the apple on the train since her rushed breakfast early that morning. Aware of Cameron watching her, she glanced across the table at him.

'What?'

He shook his head and smiled. 'I just find it wonderfully refreshing to meet a woman who enjoys her food. Far too many people are faddy about what they eat, or pander to so-called fashion in a vain attempt to achieve a body shape that's just not natural or necessary.'

'I couldn't agree more.' Ginger stared at him in amazement. To follow his own expression, she found it wonderfully refreshing to meet someone who shared her outlook on eating and health. Given her profession, and the sad stories she heard every working day, she knew how rare his attitude was and found him even more intriguing. 'So you're not one of society's many members who value thinness at all cost?'

'Hell, no! Thinness doesn't necessarily equal health or wellness. And personally I'm not attracted to skinny women.'

His voice had dropped an octave, and something about that throaty tone, along with the blatant appreciation in his eyes, made her pulse start to race and her nerves tingle with excitement. Again she remembered how he had looked at her on the train, and that made heat curl through her. She swallowed, keen to move the conversation on to less dangerous territory.

'You're in London on business?' Her change of subject caused an amused smile to curve his divine mouth and brought a reappearance of his dimple.

'Shh.' Glancing covertly around the sparsely occupied dining room, he leaned closer to her, his whisper confidential. 'Top-secret hit-man business.'

Ginger couldn't hold back the laugh that bubbled from within her, but she struggled to control her expression and whispered back. 'You could tell me, but then you'd have to kill me?'

'Exactly.' Grey eyes gleamed with appreciation and amused delight. He leaned back and took a sip of his water. 'Much as I hate to destroy the illusion, my presence here is far less exotic. I have a meeting in the morning and I'm in court in the afternoon.'

'Right.' So he was some kind of lawyer, was he? She could imagine him either bewitching or intimidating a jury or defendant. Foolishly disappointed their game had ended, Ginger returned her attention to her meal.

'What about you, Ginger? What brings you to London?'

'I have a presentation at two.'

She focused on her meal, reluctant to give too much away, knowing she could not divulge any details of the real reason for her trip or speak of her determination to succeed in winning the Ackerman funding. It was easier to maintain the pretence, to not tell Cameron what she really did or who she really was.

He pushed his empty plate aside and leaned his forearms on the table. 'Then home to Scotland?'

'Yes, and a backlog of work to catch up on.' Her gaze locked with his, and she wondered how much she dared pry. 'You're obviously a Scot, given the name, but you don't have an obvious accent.'

'My father was Scottish. He was in the diplomatic service so we moved around a lot for his job.'

She heard a trace of aloneness and dissatisfaction underlying his tone. 'That must have been unsettling.'

'It was, but I got lucky. My parents sent me back to Scotland to school at the age of eight, and

I spent the ten happiest years of my life living with my aunt outside Strathlochan. After that I lived and worked in London for many years until recently. I—' He broke off, a look of surprise on his face, as if he didn't usually talk like this to anyone. 'Aunt Kaye died three months ago.'

She ached for him and the pain of loss he couldn't hide. 'I'm sorry. She was very special to you.'

Cameron puffed out his cheeks and let out a shaky breath. 'Yes, she was. Thank you. Anyway, I have some loose ends to tie up down here.' He smiled, clearly making an effort to lighten the atmosphere.

They both had mango sorbet for dessert but refused coffee, discussing books and music and politics. Ginger was shocked how quickly the time passed and how comfortable she felt with him, despite the ever-present tingle of sexual chemistry that zinged between them.

'Well…' Realising she couldn't spin the time out any longer, she slid back her chair and rose to her feet. 'Thank you for the company. I think I'll turn in. I have a busy day tomorrow.'

'Yeah, me, too.'

It wasn't what she had intended, but she found herself walking beside him as they left the restaurant. She'd never been so aware of anyone in her life. An inexplicable tension continued to build inside her, the electricity that had charged between them from the first moment now seeming more intense than ever.

'Stairs?' She nearly jumped out of her skin when Cameron lightly touched her arm.

Glancing across the foyer, she saw that only one of the two lifts was in operation, the one they had been stuck in earlier, now carefully cordoned off. 'Definitely. All four flights of them.'

When they reached their floor, he held the door open for her, and she headed down the corridor, painfully aware he was following.

'You don't have to see me to the door,' she murmured.

'I thought we'd already decided I wasn't a gentleman.' His amused smile held a touch of wickedness. 'My room is this way, too. Four twenty-seven.'

Ginger flushed, feeling foolish. 'Of course. Sorry. Four twenty-eight.'

Her breath felt ridiculously shallow, which had

nothing to do with having used the stairs. She couldn't explain how she was feeling. They hesitated outside their doors, entry cards in hand. She knew she should just say good night and turn away, but there was something so mesmerising about him, and something weird was going on between them. Everything about him—his mouth, his eyes, his humour, his air of danger—captivated her.

Later, she could never have said who moved first. One second there was a safe gap of three feet between them, the next she was in his arms, her own wrapped around his neck, exchanging the most mind-blowing, nerve-tingling, exhilarating kiss of her entire life.

CHAPTER THREE

GINGER was on fire.

The mouth she had fantasised over since the moment Cameron had boarded the train tasted infinitely better than she could ever have imagined. Hot, male, delicious. His kiss was drugging, consuming, wildly erotic. Ginger met and matched his urgent passion, her tongue as avid in its exploration and as inquisitive as his own. She was drowning in him, lost in his heat, in the blaze of desire that raged between them. The fingers of one hand sank into the silken thickness of his hair, the other clutching at his shoulders as he drew her closer, managing to open his door and manoeuvre them both into the privacy of his room. As the door closed he leaned back against it, his hands cupping the swell of her rear and drawing her hips to his, making her gloriously aware of his arousal.

'Are you married?' she gasped, when she could force herself to drag her mouth from his.

'Hell, no.'

She whimpered as his lips worked their way along her neck, the rasp of his stubble on her skin an exciting caress. 'Living with anyone?'

'No.'

'Otherwise attached?'

'No.' Cameron's breath was as ragged as her own. 'You?'

'None of the above.'

'Thank God.'

Ginger wanted to rip his clothes off there and then. She had never experienced such an elemental need, such a desperate desire. He widened his stance and her hips settled more snugly against his. They fitted together perfectly. But it wasn't enough. She yearned for more. A terrible ache settled deep inside her, craving fulfilment, and she urgently rubbed herself against him, seeking relief. He groaned, his mouth on her throat, his teeth delivering erotic bites on her sensitive skin, his warm, moist tongue salving the delicious sting, tasting her, making her shiver with excitement.

'Are you on the Pill?'

'No.' The reality sank in. He raised his head and, eyes wide, she stared at him, unable to believe her brazenness. 'Have you got anything?'

Cameron looked tortured. 'No. I don't carry a supply around with me in case of moments like this, you know.'

Part of her was very relieved to hear it, the rest of her wanted to weep with frustration. She supposed they could ask the night porter at the front desk, or find a chemist that was open late, but that sounded too tacky, too clinical, cheapening what until then had been spontaneous, special, right. Yet the thought of walking away, of not being with him, brought a crushing wave of regret and disappointment.

Clenching her hands in the fabric of his shirt, she looked into passion-darkened grey eyes. 'What are we going to do?'

'Well...' He watched her, his smile turning naughty, his voice husky with need. 'There are other things we could do to improvise.'

Temptation curled through her at his suggestion, her imagination running riot, her pulse racing, her breath shallow as she wrestled with her decision.

* * *

Cameron was sure he would drown in Ginger's luminous, turquoise-blue gaze. She was amazing. Her sleeveless, knee-length blue dress, while not deliberately revealing, accentuated every delectable feminine contour of her body. He'd been anticipating a flowery perfume, maybe, even a spicy one, but the fruity scent of her hair and skin nearly drove him mad. He licked his lips, savouring the tang of her that lingered in his mouth. She tasted good enough to eat. Warm summer berries—ripe, juicy, succulent. His throat tightened, his stomach tightened...other parts of him tightened.

Her skin, flushed now with desire, was as peachy soft to the touch as he had imagined it would be, her hair like finest silk against his fingers. And kissing her was sensational. He closed his eyes, reliving the moment he had set his mouth to hers as he had longed to do, finding her honey-sweet, then gliding his lips down her throat, feeling her pulse quicken under his touch. His eyelashes lifting, he watched the emotions chasing each other across her incredible eyes, wondering if he'd shocked her or upset her by his suggestion. Desperate for this time with Ginger not to end, he wished he *was* the type to carry condoms around. But moments like this hadn't happened to him in a very long while—not since before his doomed marriage to Lisa—and he certainly hadn't expected any kind of liaison on this trip.

Now, though, he wanted Ginger more than he had ever wanted anyone in his life. Breathless, he waited for her answer.

Ginger was shocked at her own behaviour. She had never known this terrible desperation for someone, had never acted this recklessly in her life. If Cameron hadn't thought to ask if she was on the Pill, it might already have been too late, they would have carried on where that humdinger of a kiss had led them. Rooted to the spot for what seemed an age, a gamut of emotions churned inside her.

Was it too appallingly forward to step back into his arms and take what he was offering? She couldn't *be* much more forward, given the way she'd virtually thrown herself at the man! They knew nothing about each other. She had to be crazy to even consider doing anything like this, but she couldn't bring herself to leave him, to not experience something that felt so right.

Nerves plagued her now they had time to stop and think. Smiling, Cameron trailed the fingers of one hand down her face, leaving a tingle of fire in his wake.

'We don't have to,' he whispered. 'It's not compulsory. If you've changed your mind.'

She loved him for that, for his sensitivity and understanding. But the lightest touch of his fingers had re-ignited the hunger and confirmed how much she desired him. 'I haven't. It's not that, it's just…'

'Scary?' he finished for her when she paused, in tune with her feelings.

'Yes. You probably won't believe me but I don't make a habit of this sort of thing.' She felt compelled to explain, shivering as his fingers moved on, gliding along her neck.

'You think I do?'

'I don't know.'

'I can assure you I don't.' He brushed the pad of his thumb across her kiss-swollen lips. 'And I do believe you.'

She trembled when his fingertips skimmed the

line of her collar bones above the neckline of her dress. 'Cam.' His name escaped on a sigh and she was unable to prevent herself automatically reaching for the buttons of his shirt, slipping them undone, one by one.

Breath quickening, he waited, letting her do what she wanted. Slowly, she pulled the shirt tails free of the waistband of his trousers, then slid it from his shoulders and down his arms. She heard his breath catch as she ran her fingers over him, learning his feel, his shape. He was more than impressive, his skin warm and supple to the touch, his forearms and torso roughened with a light covering of dark hairs, more silken than she had expected. Under the bronzed skin she could feel the play of hard, well-toned muscle, and she was aware of the strength in the contours of his body. She leaned forward and set her mouth to his chest, feeling the thud of his heart, the tremor that ran through him at her touch, hearing his groan as her lips and teeth pulled gently on one responsive nipple before she traced it with her tongue. His scent was intoxicating, a heady mix of some subtle woodsy aroma she couldn't identify and his own unique maleness.

Daringly, her hands moved to begin unfastening his belt, her fingers fumbling over the task, moving on to snap open the button at the waistband of his trousers and then ease down the zip. She swallowed, her gaze clashing with his as she hesitated, seeing the heated desire in his eyes as he toed off his shoes. Tension radiated from him, but still he waited for her to make the running. Her pulse racing, and before she lost her nerve, she slid his trousers and briefs down the length of firmly muscled legs, revealing the fullness of his arousal. Facing him, she stood, trembling, hearing the raggedness of his breathing, and feeling the shiver run through him as she ran her hand down his chest and abdomen to his navel.

'You're beautiful.' Her voice was husky with a combination of desire and shyness, her hands becoming bolder as she explored lower, her fingers wrapping round him, testing him.

'Enough,' he decreed roughly.

One hand fisted in her hair, tilting her head up. His mouth met hers, as exotic and needy as before, his kiss as deeply consuming and arousing, restoking the urgency that had engulfed them the first time they'd kissed. With a whimper of desire she leaned into him, her hands playing over the exquisite planes of his back, while his own hands worked on the zip of her dress. She heard it rasp, felt him easing the fabric away, drawing her panties with it, and she stepped out of them, impatiently kicking the tangled garments away, along with her shoes. His eyes were dark with passion and appreciation as he looked at her.

Ginger quivered at his hunger, her legs shaking as he smiled, a slow, intimate smile, his fingers tracing her curves before deftly unfastening the clasp of her bra. 'Lavender lace,' he whispered hoarsely, tossing it aside, feasting his gaze on her nakedness.

An involuntary cry was drawn from her as he touched her properly for the first time, caressing, teasing, before filling his hands with the fullness of her breasts, shaping them firmly, seductively. Her nipples, already taut with longing and more sensitive than she could ever remember them, urgently pressed into his palms. Need speared through her. He bent his head, closing his mouth on one taut peak, suckling strongly. Ginger gasped at the delicious intensity of sensation.

She clutched at him, her legs giving way on her, and she sat haphazardly on the bed, taking him down with her.

Skin on skin. Cameron growled at the pleasure of having Ginger naked against him. He rolled them over on the bed until he was beneath her, his hands whispering down her back to the swell of her rear, loving the feel of her, the warm silken texture and soft, feminine curves of her luscious body. The anticipation of what was to come was a heady delight.

'Your choice.' He saw her face flush at his words. 'Whatever you want, Ginger.'

She looked down at him, turquoise eyes hot and hungry yet endearingly shy, her fingers skimming across his chest. Her tongue tip moistened trembling, parted lips. 'May I?'

Cameron nodded, not at all sure he could stand it, his breath catching as she began a slow and thorough journey with her hands and her mouth, starting at his neck and throat, then working downwards with excruciating slowness, lingering over his nipples, his abdomen, his navel. His pulse raced and his lungs felt as if they would burst. The satin strands of her hair trailing over his skin drove him mad, but not as mad as the touch of her fingers, the glide of her tongue, the edge of her teeth. He tensed as she moved down his belly and below, exploring his thighs before zeroing in on the part of him that most craved her attention. Damn, he was going to embarrass himself in a few feeble minutes!

'Ginger…'

Dear heaven, what was she doing? Every particle of his body throbbed. His heart was pounding dangerously fast and he could hardly breathe. Her sensual administrations held him captive, keeping him on the edge, teasing him, driving him crazy, before she finally led him to the most shuddering, amazing release of his life.

'You are the most wickedly exciting and exquisite woman I've ever met,' he told her when he could finally manage to speak, pulling her up and into his arms.

He brushed some damp strands of hair back from her face, his fingers sliding round to her nape and drawing her face down to his, welcoming her kiss, the sweetness of her mouth, the feel of her silken skin against his, breathing in her fruity scent. He turned her onto her back, smiling as he looked down at her.

'My turn, I think.'

Ginger looked up at Cameron, seeing the dark outer ring around the steel-grey irises of his eyes, his pupils dilated, and she was excited by the fevered intent in their depths. What she had just done, exploring his divine body, being responsible for his pleasure, had given her a feeling of sensual power. She felt almost humbled by the trust he had shown, giving her free rein to do with him as she willed. Instinctively she trusted him, too. She couldn't say why. But what was happening between them felt right, natural, as if it was meant to be.

A shiver of nervous anticipation spread through her as Cameron began his own thorough, sensual exploration of every inch of her body, assessing her reaction to each caress, learning what she liked, what made her gasp and moan and arch to the touch of his mouth and his hands. He devoted what felt like hours to loving her breasts, until she was breathless and overwhelmed, her whole body trembling with incredible sensation, and she was unable to bear any more, hovering on the brink of release.

When she thought she would tip over, he moved on, sliding down to her navel, biting and sucking on her skin, his tongue exploring, hot and moist. Her fingers clutched at his hair as she arched off the bed, protesting as he left her desperate for more. Instead, he turned his attention to her legs, starting at her feet and working upwards, a slow and sensual torture. Then he was trailing his fingers up her thighs, gliding between them, and her eyes closed as he stroked her with heart-stopping skill. Her breasts ached, her belly ached, her thighs ached. She wanted him so much, wished she could know him fully.

She moaned when she felt his mouth on the most intimate part of her. His breath was a warm caress, his lips, teeth and tongue relentless as he took her on a new, sensual journey. Again, he denied her the release she craved, keeping her on the brink, her whole being heightened with incredible sensation. Unable to help herself, she writhed beneath him, pressing herself closer, begging for more. Then her body pulsated as he did something impossible with the thumb and fingers of one hand.

'Oh, my God!' She gasped in shocked excitement as he did it again. 'Cam...!'

'Do you like that?' His husky whisper in her ear made her whimper.

She tossed helplessly on the bed, her fists clenching on the sheet beneath her. 'Oh...Cam, please.' Her breaths escaped in ragged gasps as he continued to torment her.

'Does it feel good?'

His free hand began a slow massage low on her belly where the ache was becoming unbearable. She couldn't stand it. No one had ever done anything like this to her before. He took her to the edge and held her there, driving her insane with wanting. Were those her cries? She felt wild, out of control. He had to stop. She couldn't... The intensity of sensation was shocking, the whole core of her being was on fire.

'I can't... Cam! Please...don't. Stop... Please... Oh!'

'Please stop? Or please don't stop?' he tormented, deepening the terrible, wonderful action of his thumb and fingers.

Her whole body shuddered. Her thighs were

taut, burning, trembling. She couldn't breathe, couldn't think. She was going to explode. Sobbing, she moved to the rhythm of his hands as he finally took her over the edge to the most powerful, amazing and scary climax of her life. Crying his name, spasm after spasm shook her, spiralling her away to unimaginable pleasure.

For a moment she thought she was going to pass out, then she was aware of Cameron soothing her shaking, sated body as he kissed his way back up her belly and the valley between her breasts, rolling her over, taking her with him, cradling her in his arms.

'Ginger, are you OK?'

'I'm not sure.' Still struggling to breathe, her voice sounded hoarse and croaky. An embarrassed giggle escaped and she buried her face in his neck. 'What the hell did you do to me?'

'I don't know.'

She forced her eyes open and stared at him. 'You don't know?'

'I've never done that before. It seemed like a good idea at the time,' he admitted with a chuckle.

'Bloody hell!'

* * *

'You were beautiful. Are beautiful,' Cameron praised huskily. 'Amazing.'

Ginger had been unbelievably responsive. Watching what had happened to her, feeling the reactions of her body, the wildness of her climax, had been stunning, shocking, awesome. He'd never experienced anything like it. Had never met anyone like Ginger.

'I don't think I'll ever move again,' she murmured sleepily.

Laughing, feeling an uncharacteristic warm glow of rightness deep inside, Cameron held her close for a long time, savouring her taste and scent, marvelling at her trust in him, at the magical experience they had shared. When Ginger stirred, he forced himself to release her and went to run a bath, encouraging her out of bed, supporting her when her legs threatened to give way. He lowered her gently into the water, then climbed in behind her, holding her in his arms, soaping and soothing.

Ginger sighed and leaned her head back on Cameron's chest feeling lazy and mellow. 'I think you've repositioned a few of my internal organs.'

'Are you tender? Did I hurt you?' he asked, concern in his throaty voice.

'No, of course not.' She was swift to reassure him, running her hands down his hair-brushed, leanly muscled thighs, before twining her fingers with his where they rested protectively on her stomach. 'I don't know how to explain. I can still feel it. What you did.'

She was terrified he'd do it again…shamefully, even more terrified he wouldn't. She'd never lost control like that, never surrendered herself so completely to another person. But, then, she'd never experienced such abandoned pleasure like that before, either. Had never experienced Cameron before. And they hadn't even consummated their love-making in the fullest sense of the word. She couldn't help feeling regret, wanting to know how his body would feel inside her, moving in rhythm with hers. When the water cooled, they dried each other before going back to bed, finding inventive new ways to explore and give gratification.

It was the most amazing night of her life. Erotic, sensual, extraordinary. Pip had told her to have an adventure, some fun, but she doubted her friend had ever had anything like this in mind! Finally the slept until she drifted awake to the sound of Cameron's voice.

'Ginger, it's morning. Are you OK?'

She felt the warmth of Cameron's breath fan her skin as he spoke, and her hands moved on his shoulders as he lay with his head on her stomach, one strong arm wrapped protectively and possessively around her. 'Better than OK. I just wish…'

'I know.' The fingers of his free hand traced lazy circles on her belly. 'Me, too.'

'But it was amazing.'

'You were amazing. Incredible.'

Ginger didn't dare analyse her own actions, let alone her thoughts. She'd never behaved this way before. Had never had a one-night stand in her life. Yes, she'd had her share of relationships in the last fifteen years, had enjoyed sex with a couple of long-term partners, but she had not been out with anyone since her break-up with Marc over a year ago. Never in her life had she experienced anything like the explosive intensity of passion and desire she had shared with Cameron these last hours, abandoning all inhibitions. Her body felt deliciously cherished from his thorough exploration of her, a faint redness on her skin from the exciting rasp of his stubble. She wished this time never had to end.

'Cam, did you say you had a meeting at eleven?'

'I'm afraid so.' He moved his head, licking his lips as his eyes opened and the glorious globes of Ginger's breasts greeted him. It was a sight he wished he could wake up to every day. He frowned at the realisation. 'What time is it now?'

'After nine.'

He groaned, moving so he could look at her, loving the rumpled, tumbled chaos of her hair spread across the pillow like rays of the sun, the well-kissed lips, the glaze of passion that still darkened the incredible turquoise of her eyes. 'It can't be.'

'I'm afraid it is.' She smiled, her hand stroking his face. 'Reality time.'

He couldn't explain what had happened between them. Couldn't explain the intuitive feeling that this was right. The immediacy had shocked him, yet he'd known from the first second that there was something mesmerising about this woman, something to which he was drawn on an elemental level. It sounded absurd, but it was as if some part of him recognised her, was compelled to be with her. He had never imagined there would be such a devastating out-pouring and sharing of passion. And he hadn't even experienced the pleasure of being inside her, joining their bodies in the most intimate way. Not yet.

Reality time, she had said. He couldn't ignore what he had to do today, but he didn't want to let her go, was frightened this would all dissolve like a puff of smoke if they moved, if they let the outside world intrude into this private haven of perfection they had created since they'd instinc-tively come together last night. Was it only last night? It seemed longer—yet never long enough.

He ran a hand down her body from her throat to her belly, reluctant to release her. 'You don't have to rush off, do you?'

'Not too early.' A slow, lusciously sexy smile curved her mouth. 'Whatever did you have in mind?'

Cameron chuckled. 'You're a wicked temp-tress. Come and take a shower with me.' He rolled from the bed, holding out his hand to her, leading her through to the bathroom.

It turned into a lingering delight, soaping every inch of her, feeling the slipperiness of the suds as he ran his hands over the fullness of her breasts, down the rounded curve of her belly to the swell of her rear. She was so beautiful, all feminine lushness. His breathing turned ragged as she returned the attention, his body reacting as it always did whenever she touched him. He had to see her again. It couldn't end here and now.

Dressed, shaved and ready to go, he tapped on the door of Ginger's room some while later. 'Hi.' He smiled when she answered, already feeling they had been parted too long.

'Hi.'

'I'll be finished by five,' he told her, hating that he had to go. 'I know you want to head home tonight but will you meet me downstairs before you leave? I want to see you.'

'Cam, I have to be at work tomorrow.'

'I know. Please. Just for a little while.'

'I'll see how things go.'

He tried to be satisfied with that. 'All right.

Ginger, I don't even know where you live, what you do. I want—'

'Don't.' She put her fingers to his lips. 'You'll be late.'

Terrified she wouldn't be there when he came back, he drew her into his arms, finding her mouth willing and sweetly familiar as he kissed her, deep and long and hard, trying to brand her, staking his claim with all the pent-up doubt and desperation churning inside him. She looked as flushed and breathless as he felt when he finally forced himself to let her go.

'Good luck with your presentation.' He ran his thumb over the swell of her lower lip.

'And you in court.'

Despite the urgency of his mission, he still hesitated. 'I'll see you later.'

At least she didn't contradict him. He headed down the corridor, turning at the head of the stairway and looking back, seeing her watching him. His mind in turmoil, he forced himself to walk away.

The good news was that his morning meeting had gone even better than he had hoped, and he then got away early from court in the afternoon. The bad news was that they needed him back to give evidence the next morning, so he couldn't return to Scotland with Ginger that evening. Hurrying to the hotel, he wondered how she had got on that day and whether she was waiting for him or had already left. If she had gone, how was he going to find her again? Because find her he must. No way was one night ever going to be enough with this stupendously exciting, sexy woman. He took the steps to the hotel entrance two at a time, crossing purposefully to the desk.

'Are there any messages for me?' he asked with a hopeful smile for the young receptionist.

'Yes, Dr Kincaid. Dr O'Neill is waiting for you in the salon.'

Dr O'Neill? With a puzzled frown, assuming the girl had muddled their titles, he thanked her and walked away, relieved that Ginger had come back. However, his relief evaporated when he saw the look on her face. She was pale, her eyes haunted, her hands shaking.

'Ginger, what is it? What's happened?' He drew up a chair and reached for her, concerned when she evaded his touch. 'Are you not feeling well?'

She raised bruised turquoise eyes to look at him. 'You're shortlisted for the Ackerman money.'

'What? How did you—' A terrible dread clenched his stomach with the realisation that the receptionist had not been wrong. 'Oh, no. No way. The eating disorder unit. Not you?'

'Me.'

The shock robbed him of breath. 'I had no idea.'

'Neither did I. Not until this afternoon when they let slip that the third candidate had dropped out and my only remaining competition was Dr Cameron Kincaid's self-harm facility.'

He hated the harshness and distance in her voice. 'Ginger—'

'Don't, Cameron. This changes everything.' She rose and gathered her things. 'Excuse me, I have a train to catch.'

Panic gripped him. 'Ginger, please. You can't just dismiss what's happening between us.'

'What happened. Past tense,' she corrected, and he could see the pain in her eyes, feel the answering hurt and disbelief crushing his insides as she physically and emotionally withdrew from him.

He caught her arm, desperate to detain her, disbelief making his brain sluggish, hurt paralysing him. 'It's not going to go away. Sweetheart, we can sort something out. Please.'

'We can't, Cameron. This isn't just about us now.' Ginger shook her head, moving to break the contact between them, fighting to gain the strength she needed to do what had to be done. 'We're on opposite sides now. Enemies. I can't let anything or anyone come between me and the needs of my patients.'

'I can't let my patients down, either.'

'I know. That's what I mean.'

Ginger recognised the steely determination mixed with regret in his voice. His shock had been genuine. She believed that he hadn't known the disaster that had awaited them, but she couldn't allow his arguments, his persuasiveness, her own desire for him to weaken her resolve. Her patients had to come before her own desires.

Any joy she had experienced at the success of her presentation that afternoon had been crushed with the shock of hearing Cameron's name, and the dawning realisation that he was her sole remaining competition for the funding that would mean the success or failure of her project and affect the well-being of the patients who depended on her. How could she take her own pleasure in him when the achievement of one of them would ultimately destroy the other? She had to think of the wider issues at stake, not of herself, her own selfish wants.

'Listen, Ginger—'

'No. I can't. Your victory would mean disaster for my patients and put an end to all my hard work and dreams to fulfil their needs. I'm sorry. We can't do this.' Her voice trembled, threatened to break. 'It's over. Goodbye, Cameron.'

Forcing herself to move while she still could, Ginger turned and headed for the exit, the image of his pain and shock imprinted on her brain. Tears blurred her eyes but she blinked them away, ignoring the hurt confusion in Cameron's despairing voice as he followed her and called her name one last time.

'Ginger…'

Blindly, she stepped into the first taxi on the rank outside the hotel and closed the door with a thud, separating herself for ever from the only man who had ever touched her heart and her soul.

CHAPTER FOUR

'I WISH I was dead.'

'I hope you don't mean that, Tess.' Ginger frowned as she observed the tear-stained face of the painfully thin, dark-haired girl opposite her. 'Things seem bleak and lonely at the moment, without hope, but we shall do everything we can to help make those feelings better. If you'll let us and work with us.'

The fifteen-year-old wiped the back of her hand across her face, smudging her already running mascara. 'I don't know.'

Ginger handed her another tissue and watched as the girl shredded it in her lap, her dark eyes awash with misery. She never failed to be moved by the stories of pain and despair the young people who came to her confided. It was up to her to change that, to give them new hope for a brighter future. Not that it was easy. It wasn't. Far from it. The kids were often misunderstood, angry, frightened, reserved, anxious, even rude and aggressive, but they had in common a desperate need to be helped and cared about. Ginger refused to let them down, and her growing list of success stories uplifted her patients and colleagues alike, and kept them going despite the odds.

The sight of the young girl and the knowledge of the importance of the job confirmed once more she had done the right thing by walking away from Cameron in London four days ago. The pieces of her shattered heart twisted painfully. Unable to bear the hurt that threatened to tear out her insides, Ginger tried to thrust him from her mind and focused her attention on the troubled teenager.

'Nobody likes me,' Tess confided.

'What makes you say that?'

'There's nothing to like.'

Ginger steepled her fingers under her chin. 'Why is life so bad right now, Tess?'

'Nothing I do is ever right.' The girl sniffed, unable to meet her gaze. 'I'm never good enough, I don't deserve anything.'

'How do you see the role food plays for you?'

Tess frowned. 'It's the only thing I can control. The only thing my parents can't dictate.'

'And what do you see when you look in the mirror?' Ginger probed.

'Someone useless who isn't worth anything,' she whispered.

Ginger glanced down at Tess's file and read the letter from Dr Nic di Angelis, the GP who had made the referral. This was about self-punishment, Ginger realised. The girl was seriously underweight, not because she had a distorted body image but because she believed she had no control over her life, couldn't fulfil her parents' expectations, and deserved nothing better than to waste away.

There were so many triggers for eating disorders, each as individual as the person involved and the treatment needed to help them. It could be anything from divorce to bullying, trauma to illness, loss of a loved one to family discord, an unending list of reasons why some young people responded to conflict and emotion in dangerously inappropriate ways.

'Have your periods been affected, Tess?' she

asked, jotting down some notes. 'Have they stopped altogether?'

'They've stopped,' the girl admitted, her face flushing.

'OK. And can you tell me about your eating?'

'I have regular times and set things,' Tess began slowly, and Ginger nodded, recognising the pattern and the way anorexic patients were often organised and disciplined, exerting control over their eating habits and establishing rituals and regimes. 'In the morning I have half a banana at exactly eight o'clock before school.'

'Do you eat anything during the day?'

Tess shook her head. 'I tell my parents I've eaten at school so I'm not hungry when I get in, but I haven't had anything all day except maybe some water or a diet drink.'

'What do you do then?' Ginger was careful to keep her voice light and non-judgemental. 'Do you eat anything else in the evening?'

'I'll have an apple, or sometimes a tomato, but it has to be at the right time. I sneak it up to my room, cut it into even pieces and have it at exactly eight o'clock when I'm doing my homework.'

It was no wonder she was so pale and thin,

Ginger thought. 'What happens if you have to eat at other people's houses or with your family?'

'I try to avoid it as much as possible.' Tess paused, continuing to shred the paper tissue. 'It makes me feel bad if I have to eat.'

'Physically bad? Does it hurt or make you feel sick?'

'A bit. There's a sense of uncomfortable fullness. Mostly it just makes me angry that I've lost control, especially if it is something that I've enjoyed the taste of,' she confessed.

Meeting the shy, dark gaze, Ginger smiled in encouragement, knowing how stressful this first session was when someone faced up to their troubles, often for the first time. 'You're doing really well, Tess. Can you tell me what happens afterwards, if you've had to eat a proper meal?'

'I hate myself.' The admission was delivered in a hoarse whisper. 'I shouldn't have eaten it, I don't deserve something nice, so I make myself sick to punish myself.'

As always, Ginger felt a welling up of sorrow when she heard the pain and loneliness hidden in the words. 'OK, Tess. I think we've done enough for today. I really want to help you—if you're prepared to work at it, too. But you know things are not going to get better overnight?' Ginger warned, knowing this was a two-way partnership between her team and the patient.

Tess nodded, anxiety evident in her voice. 'What will happen?'

'You'll come back and see me on a regular basis. We'll talk more, work through the things you are feeling and why, then decide what we can do to change that and make you feel better about things, including food. And we'll find other ways to cope with problems and regain control over your life and your eating,' she explained. 'You'll also see my colleague, Pip Beaumont, on each visit. She's a nurse and really nice, you'll like her. She'll help you with keeping a diary to record your emotions and what you are eating, she'll monitor your weight and blood pressure, that kind of thing, and help you with any other problems or queries you have. And you'll also see Andrew Hodge, who's a dietician. He's very understanding and he's going to help you plan a better way of managing your food to keep you healthy.'

There was vastly more to it, of course, but Tess

didn't need the added pressure at this stage. There would be weeks, months of hard work ahead, with no guarantee of a happy outcome. The statistics for recovery from eating disorders made sorry reading. While a third of patients achieved a healthy recovery and another third succeeded in managing their condition most or part of the time, the final third failed altogether, going on to develop worse problems, even losing their lives.

Just like Dee, her older sister, whose tormented teenage years had made such an impact that Ginger had been determined to devote her life to helping other people with similar problems. Sometimes it felt like she was bashing her head against a brick wall, but no way was she giving up. Every success was a joy and made all the hard work and frustrations worthwhile. She owed it to Dee's memory, to all the patients like Tess who needed her and trusted her, not to give up and to devote all her time and energies to helping them not end up a sad, forgotten statistic.

Aware her schedule was already shot to pieces, Ginger nevertheless refused to stint on the time Tess needed during this first, important appointment. 'I'm sure it all seems very daunting at the moment, but we'll do everything we can to help you, Tess. Will you work with us?'

'I'll try.' The girl gave a tearful attempt at a smile.

Ginger smiled back. 'Excellent! Now, I'll see you again on Friday when our real journey together will begin. We'll have another chat and I'll introduce you to Pip and Andrew so they can start working with you to find a programme you are comfortable with, OK? Good. Let's go and find your parents,' she finished, standing up and showing the waif-like youngster out of her room.

'Everything sorted out?' Mr Carstairs asked with false jollity, rising from a chair in the waiting room, wiping a monogrammed white handkerchief over his bald head, evidence of the effects of the summer heat combined with the stress and embarrassment of the circumstances.

'Will you take this note to Reception, Tess? They'll give you an appointment card for Friday.' Ginger handed the paper work to the girl. 'Thank you.'

When she was out of earshot, Ginger turned to the parents. She had not forgotten how rude Mr Carstairs had been to her assistant, Sarah, or his gruff and unhelpful attitude when she had spoken with him on the telephone on her return to the office last Friday. At least she had persuaded him to bring Tess for the appointment today, but she couldn't let the girl's parents think it was all plain sailing and far from serious.

'Can you help Tess?' Mrs Carstairs demanded without preamble.

'I hope so. It's not an exact science and there won't be miracles overnight,' Ginger cautioned. 'There will be a lot of hard work, not least for Tess. She needs to know she has understanding and support.'

'We don't know why she's doing this to us.' Mr Carstairs shifted from foot to foot, puzzled and angry. 'Tess has never been any trouble before.'

Ginger curbed a flash of irritation. 'Tess isn't doing this to you. She's not being naughty or vain or difficult or silly. She has an illness and she's hurting emotionally. If we don't help her now, she could become very ill indeed.'

Tess may have been given everything money could buy but what the girl needed and wanted most of all was some love. From what Nic di Angelis had told her, and she had been able to piece together from Tess today, the parents had high expectations in terms of academic achievements and future prospects, dismissing the girl's own dreams and wishes, leaving her feeling overwhelmed, unheard and unable to measure up. With low self-esteem, feeling swamped and ignored, Tess had responded by punishing herself and exerting control in the only area she could—her food intake.

'Your daughter is pretty and intelligent, but she is also very unhappy and lacking in self-worth,' Ginger continued, watching for Tess's return to ensure she did not overhear the discussion. 'It means a commitment from you to bring Tess to us once a week for the regular appointments she needs. Sadly we have no residential places at the moment.' Another reason why she was so angry at the department closure next year and doubly determined to open her own clinic. 'We have a good success rate here and we'll do everything we can to help Tess.'

'Thank you.' Mrs Carstairs was clearly taken aback, the seriousness of her daughter's situation slowly sinking in.

Mr Carstairs cleared his throat, a frown of dissatisfaction on his face. 'Friday, is it, you want to see Tess again, Dr O'Neill?'

'That's right.' Ginger smiled as Tess rejoined them, her movements slow and listless. She rested a hand on the girl's narrow shoulder and gave her a reassuring squeeze. 'Friday mornings at ten o'clock, weekly for the foreseeable future. We'll need longer for the first few appointments as Tess will be meeting more of the team who will be working with her and setting up a treatment programme.'

'What about school?' Mr Carstairs posed a further complication, showing his doubt about Tess's need for help. 'I don't want Tess falling behind with her academic work.'

Reading the girl's tension under her hand, Ginger remained calm but firm. 'I'll talk with Tess's head teacher in strictest confidence, but we've never had any problem with schools being unwilling to cooperate in helping improve health and well-being.'

'Thank you, Dr O'Neill.' Mrs Carstairs flashed a glare at her husband. 'We'll do all we can. We want our daughter to be well, too.'

Hoping harmony would prevail and they would

all be working together to support Tess, Ginger watched as the unhappy family left. There was a long road ahead and today was just the first step on that journey. Returning to her room, Ginger made a few more notes to discuss with her team before Tess returned on Friday and then called in her final appointment of the morning, hoping she could regain her focus and banish the painful images and thoughts of Cameron that were a constant distraction.

Head down, lost in thought, Cameron made his way back to his car. It was Wednesday, exactly a week since he had first seen Ginger on the train to London and his life had irrevocably changed. He couldn't get her out of his mind. He had been through an unhappy marriage and acrimonious divorce, he had suffered an unimaginable loss from which he'd wondered if he would ever recover, but he had never experienced the kind of disappointment and soul-deep ache that had been with him since Ginger had walked away from him.

Was she right? Did the fact that they were both vying for the Ackerman funding for their respective projects make them enemies? He shook his head. Competitors, yes, but never enemies. They could have worked, if only she had believed, if she had wanted it as much as he did. It was true that he had refused to consider another relationship after the debacle with Lisa, and commitment was out if it meant his personal life impinged on his work—his patients were the main focus of his life. He had never intended to get involved with a woman again, not seriously. But all that had been before Ginger. She was different, special, and the pain of being without her, of never seeing her again, making love with her, laughing with her, was too much to bear, making him question his rigid rules.

He glanced up at the small maternity unit he had just visited, spying Iain watching him from an upstairs window, and he waved before he climbed into his car. Maxine had finally given birth to a healthy baby boy with a powerful set of lungs and a fuzz of red hair on the crown of his head. They made a wonderful family. Cameron shied away from his memories, thankful that Iain and Maxine had been so engrossed in Harry's arrival that they had failed to notice his own distraction and unhappiness.

Sighing, he started the car and exited his parking space, sparing a glance at his surroundings. The maternity unit was only a decade old and sat in its own grounds adjacent to the main hospital. Strathlochan had grown beyond recognition over the decades with a rising population and now served the town residents, as well as a large and widely dispersed rural area, taking pressure off hospitals in places as far away as Edinburgh, Glasgow and throughout the southern and Border regions. The main hospital provided a comprehensive range of care and services through numerous and varied departments and clinics, including a busy A and E department. He would start work here on Monday, affiliated to the psychological services unit, conducting part-time consultations alongside his private patients and his self-help groups until his own facility was up and running.

He had more than enough on his plate to keep him busy and he could not let his focus slip. He would never forget why he was doing this, why he had left the trauma department and dedicated his life to working with and helping patients who harmed themselves. Nothing and no one had ever threatened that focus before…so why could he still not put Ginger O'Neill out of his mind? She haunted his every waking moment and fired his dreams by night. But Ginger was gone. Somehow he had to get over her, had to shut out the pain and ignore the memories of the most erotic and amazing night of his life. He needed to get his head together and put his patients before his own raging desire for the beautiful, sexy woman who had rejected him.

'Ginger, are you all right?'

She glanced up to see that the concern in Pip's voice was matched by the frown on her face. 'I'm just a bit tired,' she lied.

'That trip to London last week seemed to take an awful lot out of you,' her friend fretted. 'Are you sickening for something?'

'I'll be fine.' If she ignored her broken heart, and the fact that she couldn't sleep at night because Cameron invaded her dreams.

Her plan to throw herself with even more force and commitment into her work certainly hadn't helped so far. Every moment stretched painfully slowly and full of hurt. Why had she met someone so wonderful and perfect only to have him turn out to be the one man she could never be with? It wasn't fair. It was Friday, eight days since she had last seen Cameron and the hurt and disbelief etched on his face as she'd walked away from him for ever. The eight longest days of her life. Not only had she left behind the one man who had driven her mad with desire, she had found out he was her sole competition for the funding she so desperately needed. She was still dazed, shocked, bemused...and eight days on she had still not succeeded in pulling herself out of that befuddled state.

Renewed pain lanced through her. She had to try and look on what had happened with Cameron as a fairy-tale interlude, something magical that many people never experienced. The memories had to sustain her, because she wouldn't see him again. But it hurt so much. She still wanted him so desperately. And she hadn't even been able to experience the full intimacy of being with him, joined completely. Now she would never know what it was like to really make love with him.

'Ginger?'

'Sorry?' Pip was still frowning, she discovered, and she searched for something that would divert her friend's attention. 'I was thinking about Tess Carstairs. I'm worried about her. It's going to be a long struggle if she has so little support and understanding at home. Any more thoughts about her?'

Cradling her mug of tea, Pip sat down. 'I liked her. She's intelligent but very sad—under a lot of pressure, from what I could tell.'

'That's my impression, too. It's not a body image thing with her, is it?'

'I don't believe so. She seems almost unaware of her looks, it's all about punishing herself for not being what her parents want her to be—maybe an element of punishing them, too, for the pressure they put on her. When I talked with her, I had a sense she wanted to hold on to childhood when things were easier and less was expected of her to achieve and succeed,' Pip offered, her brow knotted in concentration. 'She doesn't seem to be able to talk to her parents at all about her own needs. Instead, they are propelling her towards a life she doesn't want and her anorexia and episodes of bulimia are her cry for help, her way of exposing her inner pain.'

Ginger nodded in agreement, her own assessment of the teenager mirroring Pip's. 'I'm worried she'll end up in hospital if we can't sort out her eating fairly quickly. She is seriously underweight.'

'Yes, I know. Andrew spent a lot of time with her today, talking about food and nutrition and encouraging her to adopt a more sensible eating pattern. I'll be interested to review her weekly diary next Friday,' Pip added, getting up and crossing to the sink to wash her mug.

'With Tess we need a combined approach, building up her self-esteem, helping her to confront her emotions and to discuss her issues with her parents. She needs to assert her own plans for her future, as well as regulating her eating and restoring herself to a normal weight. One goes hand in hand with the other. We'll need to do some work with the parents, too.' Ginger sighed, removing the clips from her hair and running her fingers through the flyaway strands. 'I wish we had the facilities available here to have her in for residential care. We could achieve so much more.'

'When do you think you might hear about the

Ackerman money?' Pip probed, her gaze sharp as she took her seat again and turned the conversation back to the new clinic.

Ginger stared down at her untouched drink, fighting a new surge of emotion. 'It will be a while, I think. They said they wouldn't be making a decision in a hurry.'

'What was he like?'

'Who?' Her voice sounded sharp and unnatural to her own ears and she struggled to control it.

'The generous benefactor! Who did you think I meant?'

Ginger's cheeks warmed at Pip's teasing. 'Sir Morrison Ackerman was interested in what I had to say but he gave nothing whatever away. Neither did his staff of lawyers and whoever else all the people were. It was so nerve-racking, Pip, like walking into the lion's den.'

Had Cameron felt that, too? Had he stumbled with nerves over the first part of his presentation as she had done? She doubted it. He was so confident and composed, she couldn't imagine anything fazing him—and yet he'd been far from composed and confident the last time she had seen him, hadn't he? Then his grey eyes had been dark with pain, his throaty voice full of despair, a tortured expression on his face. Ginger sucked in a breath and stared unseeing out of the window at the hospital's inner courtyard.

'And what about this Dr Kincaid?'

Pip's unexpected question sent a fresh jolt of pain through her. 'What about him?'

'You seem very tense and defensive whenever his name's mentioned.' Pip watched her closely, making her uncomfortable. 'Did something happen between the two of you?'

'Of course not. I only met him briefly, and I didn't realise who he was at the time,' she prevaricated, spinning half-truths.

'You got stuck in the lift together!'

She didn't want to be reminded of that night. 'Not for long, thank goodness. I'm not very keen on confined spaces.'

'And you said you had dinner,' Pip continued, apparently determined to draw out every torturous detail.

'The hotel insisted.'

'I'm not meaning to badger you, lovey, but you've been so strange since you came back, I'm worried about you,' the intuitive, motherly nurse admitted. 'This Dr Kincaid seems to have upset you.'

'Well, he wants the money I need, doesn't he?' Ginger hoped the funding issue would satisfy Pip. 'The lump sum being talked of, and the annual income for running costs thereafter, is vastly more than I could ever have dreamed of. It will mean this project could really go ahead— if we are chosen. Dr Kincaid wants to win it as much as I do.'

'Was he horrible about it?'

'No, not at all.'

No way was she telling Pip how fantastic Cameron had been, neither could she even hint at what had happened between them, that she had enjoyed the most incredible night of her life doing amazingly erotic things with a man she didn't know. She had never done anything so appallingly reckless before, not in terms of sex and relationships, anyway. Not that they'd had a relationship. Or even full sex for that matter. And that was impossible now they were competitors on opposing sides. Somehow she had to put Cameron out of her mind and her life for good.

* * *

Her schedule had been as packed as ever over the last days of August, and she had worked relentlessly with her team to help the people who came to them with a variety of eating-related issues, from anorexia and bulimia to compulsive problems and binge eating. The first Monday in September, the heatwave having broken, leaving behind cooler nights and shorter, sunny days, Ginger hurried up the stairs at the hospital and along the corridor to her office.

'Oh, Ginger! I was getting worried,' her assistant greeted her.

'I know, Sarah, I know.' She grimaced, heading through the tiny outer office to her own room where she dumped her files on her desk. 'Any messages?'

'The usual. Nothing urgent.' Sarah followed and handed over a pile of paper notes.

Ginger cast a hasty glance through them and stuffed them in her already bulging in-tray. 'They'll have to wait until this wretched combined departmental meeting is over. What time does it start?'

'Five minutes ago.'

'Damn!'

Sarah grinned. 'You'll make it. They rarely get going on time.'

'I'll have to run. Be an angel and file those patient notes for me, please.' She sent the redhead an apologetic smile. 'And can you make a start on the letters for me? They're in the top folder.'

'Sure, Ginger, no problem.'

'You're a star. What would I do without you?'

The cheeky smile Sarah offered was a good example of how far the shy young woman had come in the last months. 'I've no idea!'

Feeling a glow of satisfaction that the gamble she had taken on Sarah had paid off in the way the girl had blossomed and developed into an efficient and loyal assistant, Ginger hurried upstairs, her good humour fading as she considered the meeting that lay ahead. They'd been warned this would be a longer and broader gathering than usual and she hated being away from her work and patients. With the cancelling of her funding and closing of her unit, it was imperative to fit as much as she could into the next months—and win the financial backing from Ackerman.

The room was packed when she arrived and the

director of services was already on her feet and speaking. Spotting Pip, who had saved her a seat near the back, Ginger inched her way across.

'Sorry,' she whispered to her friend.

Pip looked at her oddly, but the director was continuing her speech. 'And we'll be benefiting from his skills on a part-time basis for the next few months. In the meantime, as well as holding his own private clients, he'll be taking on specialist cases where required, and will be available for any department requiring any advice or input.'

Ginger frowned, having missed the first part of the introduction. 'What's going on?' she whispered to Pip, trying to catch up.

'You've not noticed?' the older woman commented with a curious smile.

'What?'

Ginger glanced to the front where the director was standing behind a table, flanked by three other people. Her eyes widened in horror. It couldn't be Cameron sitting there. Her brain had to be playing tricks on her. Then, across the distance that separated them, her gaze clashed

with a compelling grey one and she could feel
the blood draining from her face.

'Oh, my God. No!'

CHAPTER FIVE

GINGER could see, hear, think of nothing else. Her only awareness was being in the same room as Cameron again, remembering his touch, his taste, the raging inferno of passion they had shared in London. This couldn't be happening. The breath was sucked from her lungs under his intense scrutiny, her blood thundering through her veins. Dimly she became aware that Pip was nudging her, and that the others in the room had turned to stare at her.

'Ginger!' The clinical director sounded impatient, and had clearly called her before. 'Are you with us today?'

'I'm sorry,' she murmured, her face flaming.

'I was suggesting you arrange a meeting with Dr Kincaid. You could find he has some useful insights for your unit.'

'We'll see.' It wasn't very polite but better than the 'not bloody likely' that had first burst for freedom and been barely restrained.

No way was Cameron muscling his way in on her patch. It was bad enough that he was fighting her for the funding she so desperately needed. She met and matched his enigmatic, unsmiling stare. Just because his touch electrified her and he happened to be sensational in bed and the sexiest man in the galaxy, it didn't mean she was going to allow him to win that money and end her dreams. Her patients, staff and other backers depended on her. She couldn't fail them.

As the meeting came to an end, Ginger made sure she was the first one out of the room, and she all but ran towards the stairs, desperate for the sanctuary of her office.

'Ginger, hold on, lovey.' Pip panted after her.

'I'm late for appointments.'

'That was *the* Dr Kincaid, I presume?'

Sighing, Ginger nodded. 'Yes, I'm afraid it was…is.' Her insides knotted with tension and pain. If only she had never had to see him again she might, just might, have been able to cope. Cameron turning up here was a disaster.

'You said he was an older guy with grey hair!' Pip accused as they walked down the stairs.

'He looked older,' she fibbed, 'and his hair is greying at the temples.' Half a dozen strands of it. 'We didn't exactly exchange personal details.'

Just rather too many other personal and intimate things. Not that she was ever going to tell Pip, or anyone else, about that!

'He is impossibly good-looking.' Pip's appreciative sigh grated on her nerves.

'You're disgustingly happily married with five strapping sons!'

'Which doesn't mean I'm blind.' Pip chuckled and nudged her with her elbow. 'I know you've not dated for a while, not since you broke up with Marc. You work too hard, Ginger. Don't tell me you've lost the ability to appreciate a good-looking man.'

'Look, can we just drop the subject, please?'

Hazel eyes regarded her shrewdly. 'What's wrong?'

'Nothing. Everything. Oh, hell!' she exploded, as she went into the office, startling Sarah who looked up in surprise. She fabricated a smile for the young woman. 'I'm sorry. Messages?'

'A few.' Sarah handed them over.

'Thanks. I'll deal with them at lunch. I must get downstairs for my appointments.' Frowning at the notes, unnerved by the turn of events, she tossed the slips on her desk and collected her files and diary. 'Sarah, if Dr Kincaid happens to ring, please don't put him through or give him any information. Tell him I'm busy with patients, visiting Mars, anything. Thank you.'

'What was that about?' Determined as ever, Pip accompanied her down to the ground floor where their outpatient clinics were taken.

'I don't know what you mean.'

'Come on, Ginger. You said yourself you and Dr Kincaid had no idea you were going for the same funding.'

'That's beside the point. And he certainly doesn't have to turn up here, poaching on my territory!' Looking so gorgeous and sexy and driving me mad with lust, she added silently.

Pip's scrutiny sharpened. 'Something more is going on here, isn't it?'

'No, of course not.' Ginger tried to laugh it off, but she could feel her face flushing.

Pip was an excellent nurse, wonderful with the

people who came to them for help, and a great friend, but she was like a bloodhound on the scent when something caught her interest.

'So, what…?'

Ginger didn't hear a word Pip went on to say. Coming along the corridor towards them was Cameron. Oh, hell. Dressed in dark trousers and a light grey shirt, he looked good enough to eat. Familiar heat curled inside her. She swallowed, her heart thudding, unable to focus on anything but him closing the distance between them, and the intense, intimate look in his eyes. He stopped in front of her and they just stared at each other for endless moments. Dear heaven, he was divine. Her gaze slid traitorously to his mouth and back up again, finding his eyes liquid with answering desire.

'Hello, Ginger.'

'Cam.' She swallowed, struggling to speak, his throaty voice sparking a fever of need inside her. Belatedly, she remembered they were not alone. 'Um, this is Pip Beaumont, mental health nurse. Pip—'

The older woman's hazel eyes twinkled. 'I know who he is! Nice to meet you, Dr Kincaid.'

'Cameron, please.' He smiled politely and shook hands, but his gaze switched back to Ginger.

Again time seemed to stand still as they stared at each other, neither speaking, both aching to touch, to kiss, to push reality away, to be back in the fantasy world they had shared that one unforgettable night. They didn't need words, their eyes seemed to speak for them.

We have to work this out, Ginger.

It's impossible.

I want you.

I want you, too.

I remember what it felt like to touch you.

I remember the feel of your mouth, your hands, your taste...

For one heartbeat she thought they swayed towards each other, and then his pager beeped, the loud intrusion snapping them back to their senses. Cameron took a step backwards, the sexy pout of his mouth almost making her weep.

'I'm on my way to Casualty.' He looked at her, his grey eyes full of need and regret. 'I have to go.' His gaze swung briefly to her colleague. 'Good to meet you, Pip.'

The older woman grinned. 'Likewise.'

'Ginger, we have to talk.'

She struggled to marshal her defences. 'No, I—'

'Please.'

'But—'

'I'll be in touch.' Cameron's parting words sounded more threat than promise.

Ginger's protest died as he strode away, her gaze following him, seeing him turn for one last look before he disappeared round the corner. She tried to suck air back into her parched lungs. Glancing down, she found her nails had carved crescents in her palms where she had clenched them in a desperate attempt not to reach for him.

'Wow!' Pip exclaimed, open-mouthed.

Ginger's pulse roared in her ears. 'Sorry?'

'I thought you were both going to spontaneously combust.'

'What?'

'Come on, Ginger, I've never seen *anything* like that! The two of you were all but ripping each other's clothes off!'

Heat washed her face as she remembered how they had done precisely that. 'Don't be silly,' she protested hoarsely.

Goodness, she needed to sit down. She opened the door of the consulting suite she used for her patient appointments and sank to her chair, dropping her files on the desk and pressing the heel of one hand to her sternum where a terrible knot of tension seemed to have lodged.

'I'm not surprised you're sitting.' As tenacious as ever, Pip followed her inside. 'If any man had ever looked at me that way, let alone such a sexy one, I'd have melted on the spot! Or ravished him!'

Ginger's blush intensified.

'Oh, my!' Pip gasped with shocked delight. 'Ginger, you didn't?'

'I may have sort of kissed him.' The admission came reluctantly because she knew Pip wouldn't give up, but she was determined not to reveal any further information.

'Sort of?' Her friend leaned her elbows on the desk, eager for details. 'What does *sort of* mean?'

'Pip, we have patients waiting. I need to get to work.'

'Something else happened, didn't it?'

And how! 'Just forget it, please.'

'Did you sleep with him?'

'Pip!'

'It wouldn't be so terrible. Far from it, I should imagine! Did you?'

'No.' Well, she hadn't, Ginger reasoned. Not exactly. There had been very little sleep involved in the proceedings and they hadn't consummated things in the way Pip was thinking. And now she was thinking about it again, she felt all hot and unnecessary. It wouldn't do. She had to focus. Determinedly, she squared her shoulders. 'Work, Pip.'

Her friend sighed with disappointment. 'OK, OK, I'm going. But you know I'm here if you need to talk.'

'I know.' Pip might get over-enthusiastic about things, but she had a heart of gold and had been a loyal friend and colleague. 'Thanks.'

Grateful to be left alone, Ginger tried to compose herself and get ready for her first consultation…but all she could think about was Cameron.

He was here, in her hospital.

What was she going to do?

Cameron made his way to Casualty in a daze. His shock when Ginger had walked into the meeting room that morning had been mirrored by the expression on her face when she had looked up and seen him. For several moments he had thought his heart would stop, that he could no longer draw air into his lungs, then his pulse had started thudding madly, the blood rushing through his veins. He had no idea what the department director had said because all his focus had been on Ginger, the way her face had paled, the lack of welcome, her barely polite response when she had been advised to meet with him.

Bumping into her in the corridor just now had been another surprise. Wearing the kind of floaty skirt that he was coming to associate with her, this time in various shades of green and blue, and a long white shirt that masked the lush fullness of her breasts from his view—if not from his memory—she had looked delicious. Her sunny blonde hair had been tied back in a loose braid, exposing the curve of her neck, making him remember what her skin had felt like, how she had tasted. And the hint of her fragrance, ripe summer berries, had teased him mercilessly. Had they been alone, had his pager not sent out a summons, he didn't think he would have been able to stop himself reaching for her and kissing her with all the pent-up longing that had raged inside him since she had left him in London.

Ginger! She was just like her name—hot and spicy. He would never forget how special things had been between them. No matter how many times he tried to tell himself it was just sex, he didn't believe it. It had been too intense, too… He couldn't even find the right words to explain it to himself—he just knew that he had never experienced that earth-shattering need and passion and closeness before. And he desperately wanted to take things that last step they had been unable to enjoy that magical night.

Reaching A and E, he forced himself to push his disturbing thoughts away and concentrate on the reason he had been called down. He glanced around the busy trauma department, feeling a momentary flash of regret for all he had given up, remembering the buzz of adrenalin he had experienced working under pressure, never knowing what was going to come through the door next. But it had been his decision to leave. The only decision…because of Molly.

'Can I help you?'

He glanced round and saw a petite nurse with

short, bleached blonde hair and hungry brown eyes looking up at him. Instinctively, he took a step back. 'I'm Dr Kincaid. I was called for a consult.'

'Oh, yes, I think that's for Dr Webster's patient.' She smiled, her gaze appreciative as she looked him over. 'Lucky for us you're available.'

'Available for consults,' he agreed smoothly, hoping to stamp down on any unwanted attention, not remotely attracted to her obvious looks, the overly made-up face, the blatant come-on in her eyes.

'I'm Olivia Barr. It's always nice to see a new face around here. I'll be happy to show you around.'

Smothering a sigh, Cameron didn't respond to the open invitation. 'Could you tell me where to find Dr Webster, please?'

Glossy red lips pouted in disappointment. 'But—'

'Olivia, there you are!' The nurse looked furious at the interruption, but Cameron turned to greet the newcomer with a feeling of relief. Dressed in standard green scrubs, which still managed to make her look feminine, and with a stethoscope looped around her neck, the young woman doctor had a vibrant energy about her. 'There's an elderly lady in cubicle two who has a nasty cut on her head. I've checked her over, but the wound needs cleaning and stitching. Would you be kind enough to take care of her for me?'

'All right,' Nurse Barr responded with evident reluctance, her expression surly.

The bubbly doctor grinned. 'Thanks, I appreciate it. Sorry about that. Olivia can be, um, over-friendly,' she added, a mischievous twinkle in dark blue eyes as the nurse stomped away.

'I noticed. Are you Dr Webster?' Cameron asked, liking the woman, admiring her open manner, her elfin features framed by shoulder-length dark hair.

'I am. Please call me Annie, Dr Kincaid.'

'Cameron.'

She smiled at him, moving across to the desk to collect a file. 'Thank you for coming down so quickly. It was a welcome coincidence you should be here today, just when we have need of your expertise.'

'What's the problem?'

'A young man called Jamie. He was involved in an accident at work, and while we were examining him, we came across a lot of unexplained scars and wounds, some old, some quite fresh.' She frowned up at him, genuine apology in her eyes. 'I'm afraid to say we don't have the time to treat cases like this with the sensitivity they need, and sadly some of the staff lack the training in how to approach and support patients who self-harm.'

Cameron nodded. It was a problem with which he was all too familiar. Thankfully, Dr Annie Webster seemed to have more idea than most about what was involved, and she seemed to care. 'How old is Jamie?'

'Eighteen. He did admit some of his wounds had been self-inflicted.'

Many people assumed that sufferers hurt themselves as a way of seeking attention, but more often than not that wasn't true. Usually the behaviour and injuries were hidden, something they did to themselves, for whatever reason, and they never wanted anyone to know. Unless the person came forward for help, it was at times like this, when some other accident or illness occurred, that the problem was discovered.

'Has he given any indication what the motivation is?' Cameron asked, making some notes of his own.

Annie Webster shook her head. 'He's not very forthcoming. I gather he's met with some judgemental and unhelpful comments from medical staff in the past.'

'OK.' Cameron sighed, knowing such reactions were far too common. 'And what happened today?'

'He works in a factory, and he received a nasty burn to his forearm. We don't need to admit him, but he'll have to come back for further assessment. His arm has been dressed, he's had some analgesia, and we're running a drip for fluid loss and any shock. I called when I heard you were here as I hoped maybe Jamie would talk with someone who knew more about the issues and had the time to help him.' She handed over the file. 'You might like to review this.'

'Thanks.'

'Sorry to interrupt.' A tall doctor, young and attractive, with dark blond hair and a ready smile, joined them, casually draping his arm around Annie's shoulders. 'We have casualties from an RTA heading in.'

'On my way. Will, this is Dr Cameron Kincaid, the new self-harm specialist from the psych department.' Annie introduced them with a smile. 'Cameron, Will Brown, fellow A and E doctor.'

Cameron shook the man's hand. 'Good to meet you, Will.'

'Thanks. You, too.'

A siren sounded in the distance, and Annie looked round. 'We have to go, Cameron, but call on one of us if you need anything. Jamie is in cubicle six,' she added before grabbing Will's hand and hurrying him away towards the emergency ambulance bay.

Smiling, Cameron watched them go, wondering if there was something between the two doctors. Left alone, he looked through the notes Annie had given him before putting the file away and walking down the corridor to the cubicle. He needed the background, but he preferred to get a firsthand picture from the patient, to learn what he could of the individual motivations and problems, which varied from case to case.

'Hi, Jamie,' he said with a smile, stepping inside and closing the curtain behind him.

The sandy-haired young man had a ruddy complexion and a reserved expression in his cloudy green eyes. His torso was bare and Cameron could see the scars of past wounds on his abdomen, chest and upper arms, some of them still raw and angry, while his left forearm was freshly dressed from the morning's event.

Pulling up a chair, he sat down by the bed. 'My name is Cameron Kincaid. I specialise in the area of self-injury. I'm not here to judge you or tell you what to do, but I can provide you with various different options to think about should you wish to follow any of them. To give you the opportunity to make your own choices,' he explained, assessing the effect his words were having on the silent, wary young man.

'I want to go home.'

'I know. And I'm sure you can leave soon. They won't be keeping you in. But while you're waiting, will you talk to me? Anything you say is in confidence. I'm not going to tell anyone, including the hospital staff,' Cameron reassured him. 'I'm here to listen and to understand—if you feel ready.'

Jamie shrugged. 'I don't know.'

'How about I ask you a few questions, and you can answer if you want to?'

'I suppose so.'

Cameron sat back for a moment, wondering how best to reach the unhappy young man before him. Every person he saw was different, with different motivations and different needs. The skill—or luck, more often, he amended—was in assessing each individual and finding a way to work with them. Jamie wasn't hostile. He was scared, yes, both at being found out and at being in a place he tried so hard to avoid, but Cameron sensed deep sadness and loneliness. If he could gain his trust and encourage him to talk, he believed he could begin to help him find other ways of coping with his anxieties and problems.

'Have you ever talked to anyone, Jamie, about how you feel or why you do what you do?' he asked, watching the young man's face.

'No.'

'Because you don't want to, or because you think no one will understand?'

The young man shrugged again, his eyes shadowed with hurt. 'How can anyone understand? People would just hate me, think I'm a freak.'

'You'd be surprised, Jamie.' Cameron leaned forward, resting his elbows on his knees. 'You are not a freak, and people do understand. I meet people every day who say the same thing and I can assure you that you are not the only person who does what you do or feels the way you do.'

Cameron waited a moment, allowing his words to sink in. He was about to speak again when footsteps approached and the curtain was pulled back.

'Oh, sorry.' An older nurse smiled at them. 'I didn't know you had a visitor, Jamie. I just came to check your drip.' The boy retreated into his shell as the nurse satisfied herself that the fluids had finished running in, then removed the cannula and fixed a sticky plaster over the site. 'That all seems fine. I'll bring you an outpatient appointment card and some other bits and pieces, then you can go home. Have you someone you can call?'

Jamie shook his head. 'I'll be fine.'

'Well, perhaps your friend can help you,' the nurse suggested.

Cameron didn't correct her about his identity. When she had gone to fetch the paperwork, Jamie pulled on his shirt, wincing as he moved his damaged arm. The nurse was soon back, explaining the appointment and giving Jamie some medication.

'Why don't we walk along to my room? I can get some information for you and arrange for you to get home,' Cameron offered, keeping his voice light.

'OK,' Jamie agreed after a moment of hesitation. 'Thanks.'

'No problem. You all right to walk for a bit?'

'Yeah.'

The casualty department was busy coping with the aftermath of the RTA, so Cameron made a mental note to update Annie Webster later. Matching his pace to Jamie's, Cameron walked back towards the outpatient wing of the hospital, aware he was approaching the danger area where Ginger was working. He just couldn't put the woman out of his mind. Unlocking the door of the consulting room assigned to him, he showed Jamie inside and invited him to sit down.

'Is there no one I can ring who can come and collect you?'

'I don't have anyone. Not now. Mum took up with some guy a couple of years ago and he threw me out. He used to hit me…and me mum.' Cameron held his breath, hoping Jamie would continue, surprised but relieved when it all came pouring out. 'I stayed with a friend for a while but it didn't work. I've got a bedsit now. And a job. It's horrible there, though. I don't get on with people, or have any friends. And I feel bad I can't help me mum. She doesn't want to see me 'cos it will cause trouble with her bloke. I feel alone and useless.'

'Does causing yourself pain outside, help equalise the pain inside?' Cameron prompted, wary of pushing too soon but taking advantage of Jamie's apparent need to get things off his chest.

Jamie looked surprised, but he nodded, his voice unsteady. 'Yeah, it does. It makes me feel calmer. Sometimes I need to cut so badly. Sometimes I make myself wait because I think I don't deserve to feel better.'

'You do deserve to feel better, Jamie, and there are other ways of achieving that, however difficult that is to believe right now. I want to help you—if you'll let me.'

'How, though? What would I have to do?'

'Nothing you don't want to,' Cameron reassured him, knowing one wrong move and Jamie would flee. 'I think you'd find it helpful to come along to one of my evening groups. I have two a week. You can come and go as you please, but you'll meet other people who feel the same as you, people who will understand and who find it helps to talk.'

Jamie looked doubtful. 'I don't know,' he prevaricated, worriedly chewing his lower lip.

'As I say, the choice is yours.' Cameron smiled again, gathering some leaflets together. 'Why don't you come along one night and see how it goes? You don't have to say anything unless you want to, and you can always leave if it doesn't feel right for you. We can also make an appointment for you to come back here and talk to me on your own if you'd like that. I'll give you these things to read over, and next time we meet we can chat about what you think you might like to do. How does that sound?'

'Yeah, OK. Maybe I will.'

Handing over the leaflets, Cameron hid a sigh of relief. 'Great. Now, how about I organise some transport home for you?'

'Thanks.'

'No problem.'

It took a while but Jamie eventually had his ride home, and Cameron could only hope the young man would continue the brave step he had taken that day in beginning to speak about his problems. He had his fingers crossed that Jamie would come along to a group session and keep the appointment they had made for the following week. Sometimes things moved painfully slowly in his line of work but the rewards were massive when he was able to help someone turn things round and make better choices with their lives.

A stab of pain lanced through him when he recalled the one person he hadn't been able to help. Molly. He squeezed his eyes shut against the welling of emotion. He should have seen it, should have done more. But he hadn't. Not until it was way too late. And now he drove himself to make sure he helped as many other people as he could, stopped as many as possible going through what Molly had, or experiencing the ache of loss that speared his soul every day of his life.

Heading for the stairs, he wondered if he had time to grab some coffee before his afternoon appointments began. He heard footsteps a couple of flights above him and glanced up, his heart catching as he saw Ginger on her way down. His gut tightened at the sight of her. He walked on, seeing the shock mix with hurt and longing in her turquoise eyes as she met his gaze. Her steps slowed, halting when they were barely a couple of feet apart. It wasn't close enough. He wanted her in his arms, in his bed, wanted to push the rest of the world away.

'Hi,' he greeted her, hearing the roughness in his own voice.

'Hi.' He saw her suck in a breath. 'How did it go in Casualty?'

'OK. Ginger, we need to talk.'

'No, Cameron. It's too late,' she insisted, clearly panicked.

He shoved his hands in his trouser pockets, re-sisting the urge to reach out to her. 'I don't believe that. Have lunch with me.'

'I can't. I'm already running late.' She broke off as the door behind him opened and a couple of nurses came through, their chatter and laughter resounding in the stairway as they hurried up towards their ward. Her gaze met his again, her hand shaking as she tucked some flyaway strands of hair, which had escaped her braid, back behind her ear. 'I was just going to have something on the run in my office and—'

'Your office will be fine.'

'But…'

He knew that wasn't what she had meant but he wasn't about to let the opportunity pass him by. No way. If she wanted to make this some kind of battle between them, so be it, but he wasn't going to play fair, not when the stakes were so high—not when he wanted her so damn badly. The conflict that had arisen so unexpectedly between them could not be ignored, but neither could the amazing chemistry they shared. Fate had decreed their paths should cross a second time and he was damned if he was going to let Ginger get away again. Not until they had talked things out, explored all the possibilities of making this work. He yearned for her as he never had for anyone else. There had to be a way to separate their professional differences and their personal connection.

Moving up one more step, closing the gap between them, so close he could feel her heat, inhale her fruity scent, he leaned closer, his mouth a hair's-breadth from hers.

'Your office. Now… Or we do this in public.'

CHAPTER SIX

Do what in public? Ginger worried frantically.

She stared into Cameron's mesmerising grey eyes, feeling the familiar electricity fizzing between them. It was all she could do to keep her hands off him. But she had to. This wasn't just about them any more. She couldn't forget that. Hearing a few ribald comments, she glanced round, her face flushed, as a group of junior doctors went down the stairs, smirks on their faces as they looked at her and Cameron standing so close to each other. Embarrassed, she moved back up a couple of steps, putting some much-needed distance between them.

'My office,' she managed to rasp, scared what Cameron might do if she didn't agree to talk with him.

This was a very bad idea, she fretted as she led

the way along the corridor, but it sure as hell beat being found in some compromising position on the hospital stairs. She opened the outer door and found her assistant still at her desk.

'Sarah, you're here. I thought you'd be at lunch.' She cleared her throat, far too aware of Cameron close behind her. 'This is, um, Dr Kincaid.'

'Hi, Sarah.'

'Hello.'

Ginger saw the young redhead blush as Cameron smiled at her and shook hands. The man was lethal! And he wasn't even trying. Getting herself back under some semblance of control, Ginger made herself glance at him, trying to keep her manner polite and formal.

'If you would wait in my office, I just need a word with Sarah.'

'Of course.'

She sucked in a breath as he deliberately brushed the length of his body against her on his way by, his gaze holding hers long enough to convey his desire, to challenge her to deny hers. Her pulse racing, she turned her attention back to her secretary, who was wide-eyed with a mixture of surprise and interest.

'Sarah, I've just come down from Intensive Care. They've had to admit Danielle Watson,' she said with a resigned sigh. 'Can you get hold of Pip and Andrew and let them know, please? I'll see them both for a crisis meeting this afternoon.'

The young assistant nodded. 'No problem.'

'Thanks. You head off to your break now.'

'OK.' Still flushed, Sarah regarded her with open curiosity. 'Can I get anything for you?'

Ginger glanced towards her office, her heart thudding as she saw Cameron perched on the edge of her desk, watching her. 'No, that's all right, thanks. I'm already running late. I'll get a coffee while I, um, talk to Dr Kincaid,' she mumbled, her mind distracted.

Talk. That was right. That was *all* she and Cameron were going to do, she thought determinedly, pouring two mugs from the coffee-percolator Sarah kept fresh for her in the outer office. Legs like jelly, she walked into her office and closed the door, scarcely able to breathe as her gaze locked with a sultry grey one. Mutely, she handed him a mug, startled when he took them both and set them down on her desk before taking her hands in his. Instantly, the connection was made, shooting fire along her nerve endings as if she'd received an electric shock.

'Ginger...'

'We shouldn't be doing this.' Her protest was pitifully weak, and she tried unsuccessfully to resist as he drew her closer. 'Nothing changes the fact that we're on opposing sides. Unless you're going to give up applying for the funding.'

Cameron's expression was regretful but determined. 'I can't do that, Ginger.'

'Neither can I.'

'I know.' He brushed some wisps of hair back from her face. 'It doesn't mean I don't admire or support what you do, but I have my own patients and staff to think of.'

Tears of disappointment and frustration stung her eyes. 'Then we're still enemies.'

'Never enemies.' His smile brought a reappearance of his dimple, and his fingers began to trail across her face and down her throat, taking her breath away.

'Don't, Cam.'

His throaty voice was all temptation. 'Just a kiss.'

'It's never just a kiss,' she reminded him,

knowing how instantly things flared out of control between them.

'I promise.'

'You can't.' She certainly couldn't.

His hands returned to her neck, one thumb brushing across her lips, and she fought to stop herself swaying towards him, every fibre of her yearning for his touch. 'It's been for ever since I held you, kissed you,' he whispered hoarsely, the roughness of his need making her think of the last time, their farewell that Thursday morning in London. He had held her tight, and kissed her long and hard in the doorway of her hotel room…before the reality of their situation had crashed down around them hours later.

'Eleven days, three hours and…' she glanced at her watch before her hands moved to his sides, clenching in the thin material of his shirt '…nearly twenty minutes.'

'Far too long.'

Before she could protest further, his mouth captured hers. The relief. The excitement. As his fingers dispensed with her braid and locked in her hair, her arms slid round him, her lips parting in welcome. She sighed, pressing herself closer, burning with longing for this man. He leaned his hips back against the desk and slid one leanly muscled thigh between hers. Damn. She'd known it was never going to be just a kiss! How could she want anyone so much? Unable to help it, she urgently rubbed herself against his leg, seeking to assuage the desperate ache building deep inside her. It didn't work.

Tormentingly, Cameron sucked on her lower lip, and she whimpered. He nibbled with his teeth then let go, slowly increasing the pressure of his mouth, changing the angle so he took more. The kiss turned deeper, hotter. Her tongue brushed and stroked along his, and she moaned when he gave her what she wanted, his tongue curling with hers, drawing her into him. One of his hands slid beneath the hem of her shirt, his fingertips tracing circles of fire on the heated skin along her spine. A tremor ran through her and she rocked against him, her hands tightening on the broad strength of his back as she matched his every move. But then he teased her, his tongue retreating, its tip returning to lightly tickle the sensitive roof of her mouth, driving her mad. Her own tried to intervene, to stop him, and she felt him laugh, his breath huffing into her, warm and exciting. No one should be allowed to kiss this way. It simply wasn't fair. All rational thought and common sense had long since evaporated.

Finally, he drew back, cupping her face in his hands, his breath as ragged as hers. 'I like the way you do lunch,' he whispered naughtily.

'God!'

She'd forgotten everything, including where they were. Her gaze strayed to her office window, thanking fate that her room wasn't overlooked. Anything could have happened— would have happened—if he hadn't stopped. Somehow, she dragged herself away from him and made it round her desk, sinking to her chair, shaking from head to toe. She was a fool. She hated herself for losing control, for giving in so easily, for forgetting the important reasons why this could never work. For goodness' sake, she had even forgotten poor Danielle Watson, lying alone, so thin and pale and lost up in Intensive Care. Shame curled inside her. How could she have put lustful desire before patient needs? This was just what she had feared, one of the many reasons she couldn't allow Cameron to distract her.

Fighting for some sanity, she picked up her mug and sipped her now lukewarm coffee, watching over the rim as Cameron sat down opposite her.

'What are we going to do?' he asked, his intent grey gaze meeting hers.

'There's nothing we can do but stop.' Sighing, she set her mug down on the desk, hiding her hands on her lap as they were still trembling. 'If it was just me, I could walk away, but it isn't. I have to think of patients, staff, investors, backers…the same as you do, Cam.'

A distracting pout of consideration shaped his mouth. 'This thing we have isn't going to go away.'

'It's just lust,' she fabricated, shifting uncomfortably under his scrutiny.

'Is it?' His eyes turned silvery as he dismissed her words. 'I don't believe that, Ginger, and I don't think for a minute that you do, either.'

'It doesn't matter what we believe. There can never be anything between us.'

She looked away from him, trying to be strong, to do what she thought was right. Yet she was unable to deny the raging, elemental desire and unquenchable need that overtook her whenever she thought of him, saw him, touched him. He may be the enemy, but attraction flared out of control whenever they were together. How was having Cameron Kincaid on her patch going to affect her work? True, he dealt with self-harm, a different area to her, but at the very least they were bound to bump into each other from time to time. Somehow they would have to develop a workable, professional relationship, but she wasn't at all sure she could handle seeing him and yet not be with him.

On the other hand, allowing anything else to develop between them would be a terrible mistake. A brief, albeit exciting affair might get it out of their systems, but it would just make everything, especially the final goodbye, even worse. She—

'Ginger, please.' Cameron's heartfelt interruption drew her from her difficult thoughts. 'I'm not letting you walk away from me again. There has to be a way we can separate our personal and professional lives.'

'Don't you see? One of us is going to be badly

hurt when this ends—and end it must, when a decision is made about the money.'

'But—'

She held up her hand, forestalling him. 'No, Cameron. For one of us the dream is going to come true, while the other will be left with nothing. That is going to be even harder to deal with if we are involved in any way beyond the professional. I'm not prepared to take that risk. I have to put my patients first,' she insisted, knowing she had already made the painful decision once when she had walked away from him in London. It had been the hardest thing she had ever done. Could she find the strength to do it a second time?

'It doesn't have to be that way. What we have has nothing to do with the money,' Cameron countered, his determination, his nearness, and her own desire playing havoc with her resolve.

Cursing her weakness, she failed to resist him when he reached out and took one of her hands in his. 'Cameron…' She closed her eyes, unable to look at him, part of her frightened he would finally agree and walk away, although she knew that was the best thing to do, for both of them.

'In the immediate future we're bound to meet each other. There will be times we'll have to work together, here at the hospital,' he reasoned, mirroring her earlier thoughts.

'I suppose so.'

His fingers linked with hers, his thumb gliding across her wrist, distracting her. 'I really am interested in the work you do, Ginger. I'd like to know more about it.'

'Spying on the competition?' she challenged, suspicious of his change in tactics. But she regretted her words when he flinched, releasing her hand, and she saw hurt cloud his eyes.

'No, that's not what I meant at all.'

'I'm sorry.' She bit her lip, affected by the chastisement in his voice. 'That was unfair of me.'

He considered her in silence for a few moments, his expression shuttered, giving away none of his emotions. 'I've no doubt your schedule is as hectic as mine, but I was going to ask you to come and sit in on one of my evening self-help groups. I thought you might be interested.'

'I would be, thank you.' She was surprised how much she wanted to learn about his work, but she was confused at the footing they were going to be on. Could they really keep things professional? 'When do you run them?'

'Tuesdays and Fridays. I'll give you all the details. You'll come?'

'All right. Perhaps you'd like to sit in on one of our sessions some time,' she found herself offering in return, berating herself for being all kinds of a fool.

His smile reappeared, warming every atom of her being. 'Thanks, Ginger, I'd love to.'

'OK.' She was finding it hard to breathe again. She had to be mad, committing herself to spending more time with him. Struggling to keep things businesslike, she averted her gaze and controlled her voice. 'I'll ask my assistant to sort something out.'

Without waiting for his response, she tied her tousled hair back in a ponytail, gathered up her things and rose to her feet. Her gaze flicked over him and she immediately wished it hadn't. She couldn't think when she looked at him. He was so gorgeous, so sexy. And it wasn't fair that things were so impossibly complicated.

'I'm sorry, but it's late, and I have appointments downstairs,' she explained, edging towards the door. 'I have to go.'

He rose from the chair with supple grace. 'Me, too. I'll walk down with you.'

Ginger wasn't sure that was sensible but there didn't seem to be an easy way of avoiding it. She reached to open the door, hesitating when his hand closed over hers, preventing her escape. Her whole body trembled in reaction to that simple touch and she smothered a groan.

'Cam?'

His free hand cupped her chin, forcing her to look at him. Grey eyes darkened and she shifted restlessly, her exit route cut off as his body pressed her lightly back against the wall. His lips met hers, warm and sensual, starting a new inferno of need raging within her. All too soon he moved away, leaving her unsatisfied, his fingers tracing her tingling, kiss-swollen lips before he lowered his hand.

'We've done things kind of back to front, haven't we?' His smile was wry, but Ginger thought his words smacked of supreme under-statement. 'Let's get to know each other properly. We can do this, Ginger.'

Taken aback, she frowned, not sure this was what she wanted at all. 'I don't know...'

'Please. I'm not going to give up.' His voice was seductive, wearing down her defences. 'Give us a chance. A day at a time.'

Despite all her reservations, she found herself giving a brief, wary nod. She was mad to agree, for all kinds of reasons. He allowed her to open the door and they left the office, making their way down to the ground floor. Not only was it dangerous to get to know more about him and his work, to like him more, to be sidetracked from her own goals, but her feelings for him were decidedly *un*professional. She only had to be in the same room as him and she wanted to rip his clothes off!

'Ginger, I'll be here on Wednesday.' They lingered in the wide, airy foyer of the hospital outpatient reception, his loose grip on her wrist detaining her and making her pulse race. 'We'll arrange something for Friday evening. Is that OK?'

'Um, fine.' Ginger sighed, thinking it was anything but fine yet unable to help herself.

Unfathomable grey eyes looked into hers for endless moments before he released her and stepped back. 'See you.'

Ginger watched as Cameron walked away, her heart thudding, her insides aching with unfulfilled need. What on earth did she think she was doing? It was wrong to even consider seeing him again, given the circumstances and the conflict between them. They were in a competition that only one of them could win. Someone was going to get badly hurt before this was over. Seeing Cameron again, even in a professional capacity, was opening herself to even more heartache. Yet she hadn't been able to say no. She shook her head, mystified how everything had shifted out of kilter and spun so thoroughly out of her control.

Lost in thought, Cameron sat on the wooden steps that led down from the decking to the garden at the rear of the Chamberlains' cottage. Tomorrow night he would see Ginger, talk to her. At last. Provided nothing else went wrong. It had been a horribly frustrating couple of weeks. After cajoling her into agreeing to see him, and securing a promise to exchange information about each other's work, he had banked on enjoying her presence at his self-help group within a few days. Things hadn't worked out that way.

He had worried that Ginger was deliberately avoiding him, and putting him off, because Friday hadn't worked out and neither had the following Tuesday. It had been days since they had spent time together and he was panicking, desperate to see her, even if only at work. All he had managed had been the occasional glimpse of her rushing between appointments or visiting her sick patient on the ward. The chances for a chat on the run had been even fewer. As for touching her, kissing her...well, he could forget it.

He'd been far busier at the hospital than he had expected, but that just proved how much his services, and his new clinic, were needed. However, hours at the hospital were escalating until there was little time left after his private consultations and his self-help groups to work on his own project. Less still for a social life. And all the while he found himself distracted by thoughts of Ginger, watching out for her, yearning to hear her voice, to hold her, make love to her, and he cursed himself for his foolishness. There really wasn't time in his life for anything but work, yet this thing with Ginger, whatever it was, went beyond anything he had ever experienced. He couldn't give her up. Not yet. Not before they had even had a chance.

On the plus side, the last couple of weeks had delivered him an unexpected ally. Ginger's friend and colleague, Pip Beaumont, the matronly nurse, had shared a few cups of coffee with him during snatched breaks between consultations. Pip encouraged him not to give up and had let drop some interesting snippets of information. He now knew that Ginger worked ridiculously long hours and that she'd not had any kind of social life since her last relationship had ended over a year ago. Pip had also told him that Ginger's rare days off were spent indulging in some thrill-seeking sports to blow off steam. That had surprised and intrigued the hell out of him.

Yesterday, he had finally pinned Ginger down to a promise to attend his Friday group meeting. It had taken Pip's help, along with the good news that the patient she was so worried about, Danielle Watson, was out of Intensive Care and making small strides towards recovery, but, barring some unforeseen act of God, he would be seeing Ginger tomorrow evening. Thanks to Pip, he also knew that Ginger was off for the weekend on some exciting jaunt. He hoped to wangle himself an invitation to go with her. Whatever it was. Just so long as it didn't involve anything like potholing or caving.

'Here you go, Cameron.'

Iain's voice drew him from his reverie, and he glanced up, taking the bottle of beer his friend handed him. 'Thanks. And for dinner. It was great.'

'Maxine's giving Harry a feed and putting him down to sleep.' Iain sank down on the steps beside him with a contented sigh. The September evening was warm, the moonlit sky silhouetting the wooded hills across the valley. 'So, who's the woman?'

'What woman?'

'The one who has your thoughts in such a tangle.'

Cameron frowned, trailing a finger through the condensation on the outside of the cold bottle. 'What makes you think there's a woman?'

'I know you've hardly been Casanova since your experience with Lisa, but work has never put you in this kind of edgy, troubled mood.' Iain glanced at him but the smile failed to mask his underlying concern. 'What's her name?'

'Ginger.'

Iain's smile broadened. 'That's unusual.'

'She's an unusual woman.' Cameron took a pull of his drink, feeling warm inside as his thoughts returned to the woman who had dominated his existence since the day they had met. 'Ginger is feisty and fiery. She works hard and plays hard. She fights for what she thinks is right, she's loyal to her friends and colleagues, and she's a staunch champion for her patients. She's passionate and gutsy, and she cares desperately about those affected by eating disorders.'

'Wow! She's certainly made an impression on you in a very short time.'

His friend's amusement was evident. 'Yeah. I'm crazy about her, Iain.'

'That's good.'

'No. It isn't good. I can't allow anything to deflect me from getting my clinic off the ground.'

'You're the most driven person I know. I can't say I haven't worried about you, about the way you've taken this on like some kind of crusade after Molly...' Silence stretched for a few moments as Iain touched on a no-go area, and Cameron tensed, as he always did at the mention of the name. 'It wasn't your fault, buddy. You blame yourself about Molly, but you couldn't have done any more.'

'I failed her,' he said through gritted teeth, his hands tightening around the bottle.

'No, you didn't. Cameron, I admire your dedication, the way you've thrown yourself into this and taken up the battle for people who self-harm, but…'

'But what?' he demanded, unable to stem the thread of anger and unease.

Iain sighed, resting a hand on his shoulder. 'You need some balance in your life. This project is taking you over. A woman is just what you need. How crazy are you about Ginger?'

'Never-get-out-of-bed kind of crazy.' Groaning, he set down his bottle and rubbed his face with his hands. 'This is all too complicated.'

'It's amazing, that's what it is! I never thought I'd hear you talk like this about a woman again, not after Lisa.'

Cameron sobered at his friend's words. 'Neither did I. But you haven't heard the worst of it.'

'What does that mean?' Iain asked, wariness in his voice.

'Ginger is also my sole competition for the Ackerman money.'

Iain swore and his expressive comment hung between them. 'Did you know that when you met her?'

'No. Neither of us did.' Cameron closed his eyes, recalling that one magical but unfulfilled night in London.

Frowning, Iain paused for a moment's thought before he continued. 'But Ginger knows now?'

'Of course.'

'What does she say?'

Cameron let out a frustrated huff of breath. 'She thinks one of us is going to get hurt, that it's best if we don't see each other any more.'

Iain whistled. 'And what do you think?'

'That she's probably right. But I can't stop, can't let her go. I've never felt anything like this before, Iain. What Ginger and I have is explosive, special.'

'Oh, man. You sure don't do anything the easy way, do you?' Iain shook his head.

'Whichever one of us wins the funding—well, it means we prevent the other from fulfilling their dreams.' Ginger was right about that,

Cameron admitted to himself. And it was a horrible price to pay. The trouble was, the knowledge still wasn't enough to stop him needing her, wanting her. 'I'm seeing her tomorrow night.'

'Damn it, Cameron. I hope you know what the hell you're doing.'

A wry laugh escaped. Iain wasn't the only one, Cameron thought, draining his beer. Not that he'd known what he'd been doing or been in control of his senses since meeting Ginger. From the first moment he'd felt like he'd been hit by a speeding truck.

Sighing, he acknowledged that his friend was right. He *was* driven. Driven by the determination that no more families would be ripped apart, that no other parent would have to suffer the horrific pain of loss and sense of failure that darkened his days and nights. He couldn't let his patients down. Whatever it took, he would fight to ensure they received the support and treatment they needed. He knew, without a shadow of a doubt, that Ginger would do the same for those in her care. All he could hope was that, despite all the odds, they wouldn't destroy each other in the process.

The situation was no clearer in his mind the next evening. The members of his group arrived at the hall in dribs and drabs, some talking nervously, some keeping to themselves. Even Jamie, the young man he had met in Casualty his first day at the hospital, had turned up, his anxiety painfully apparent. Cameron felt on edge himself, wondering if Ginger would come, wondering what she would think of the work he did…wondering if he could hold on to her after the meeting was over and persuade her to spend some time with him.

After talking with Iain last night, Cameron couldn't help but be aware of all the pitfalls of taking his relationship with Ginger further, neither did he fail to recognise the dangerous ground he was walking on. But as the door opened and Ginger stepped inside, her flyaway hair tousled by the evening breeze, he met her pensive gaze and his heart stopped. She wore a long, multi-coloured skirt with a knee-length cardigan over a smart T-shirt, and a coat draped over her arm. She looked curvaceous and lushly feminine. His heart started beating again, far too fast, and he sucked in a much-needed lungful of air as he rose to his feet and crossed to greet her.

Aware of the curious speculation of his group members, he took Ginger's hand, trying to ignore the immediate awareness that raced through him when the connection was made, and drew her forward.

'Everyone, this is Ginger O'Neill. She's a friend and colleague who specialises in eating disorders. I've invited her to sit in. Is that all right with all of you?'

There was a hum of wary agreement and shy greetings. Cameron was conscious of Ginger's skill in putting people at their ease, and that quality was at the fore now as she focused on each person in turn, keeping things light and friendly, unfazed by the very different characters. Distracted as he was, by her presence and the very sight of her, he watched her draw up a chair into the circle and take her seat, expectation on her face as she waited for him to begin.

Ginger wanted them to keep things on a professional footing, but that had never been an option. They were fooling themselves if they thought that was going to work. The sexual chemistry was too strong, too compelling. But inviting her here, pursuing this electric connection, had to be the dumbest thing he had ever done. They were playing with fire. Before much longer they would be eaten alive by the flames and he could only hope they came out of it un-scathed—singed, perhaps, but not badly burned.

CHAPTER SEVEN

'MY NAME is Eleanor, and I'm seventeen. I don't want to die, I want to live, and that's why I do this.' The voice faltered, scared dark eyes scanning the room before she swallowed and seemed to regroup and gather her strength to go on. 'I've been cutting myself for three years and I never thought of telling anyone about it until I came here a few weeks ago. Life's really crappy, you know? Things have been bad at home. Seriously bad. I found that if I did things to myself, cut myself, it soothed the terrible inner pain I couldn't share with anyone else. It helps me go on.'

Ginger wanted to cry. She couldn't look at Cameron. Instead, she stared intently at a point on the wall behind Eleanor's head and forced herself to breathe slowly and evenly, blinking once—hard—to push back the threat of tears.

She heard some dreadful stories every day of her working life, but the bravery and the pain displayed by these young people Cameron worked with humbled and moved her.

'I find it's, like, if I bleed, I'm letting out the hurt,' an older girl said now. 'I'm Tracy. I'm twenty-one, and I dropped out of university last year. No one understood. I had everything. Big home, rich parents, everything. But they've always pushed and pushed and pushed me to follow their dreams, rather than my own. I tried to do it their way but it wasn't what I wanted, wasn't what was right for me. I started cutting and burning myself when I was thirteen. We've always had big rows but they threw me out when I refused to return to uni. But that was OK. I have my own place now, a job in a bookshop—and thanks to Dr Kincaid I'm going to art therapy classes,' she added with a shy smile in Cameron's direction. 'I like it; it helps. I find I can get my frustrations out on paper. I've not injured myself for a month… although sometimes I still feel I want to.'

A murmur of support ran around the group of a dozen very different people sitting in a rough circle in the small church hall. Cameron smiled

at Tracy and nodded his approval and encouragement. 'That's great. And how are you feeling?'

'Not too bad. I still worry about things—what
happened in the past, especially at home—but
I'm beginning to understand that there are other
ways to cope, that I don't have to do what other
people want me to do all the time, that I can find
my own way in life. And that there's a lot of life
left,' the young woman admitted, twisting her
fingers nervously in her lap.

Ginger thought of Tess Carstairs and her
family situation. The only difference between
her and Tracy was that Tess chose to starve
herself and purge anything she considered wrong
to have eaten, as a way of punishing herself and
coping with her frustrations and her pain. With
Tracy, it was causing herself external pain,
cutting and burning herself, to balance the pain
inside over which she felt she had no control.

'I'm the same.'

The hall fell silent after the whispered words.
Ginger saw Cameron's surprise as he realised
who had spoken—a young man with sandy hair
and a ruddy complexion, with one arm bandaged.
In his late teens, Ginger estimated, his anxiety

was evident in the way he rocked himself back and forth, his whole body trembling.

'Do you want to tell us how you feel, Jamie?' Cameron sent the young man a smile of understanding. 'You don't have to, but we're here to listen when you are ready to talk.'

'I don't kn-know if I can,' Jamie stumbled.

Cameron nodded. 'That's all right.'

The girl called Tracy, who seemed to have come the longest way on her journey to recovery, as far as Ginger could tell, leaned forward to smile at the young man. 'We all felt like that, Jamie. It takes us all time to feel comfortable to talk.'

'I didn't think there were any other people like me.' He looked around the group, his green eyes dark with fear and confusion. 'When Cameron… Dr Kincaid…suggested I come here, I thought it would be a waste of time. That you'd all think I was a freak.'

'Nobody thinks that, Jamie,' Cameron reassured him.

'Not at all,' Tracy agreed. 'It's the same for each of us.'

Eleanor sat forward, her expression earnest and sincere. 'We're all survivors, aren't we?

Because we are here. Talking helps. Knowing we are not alone. It isn't always easy, but we've all faced the same kinds of things, we understand what it is like.'

Other members of the group joined in with their support and the conversation moved on to individual experiences, what had led them to begin harming themselves, how they did it, and the ways in which Cameron was trying to channel their emotions and energies to other things. Like art therapy for Tracy. What became clear was that, contrary to general misconception, the majority of people who self-harmed were not attention-seeking and not trying to kill themselves—rather, they were fighting to live, coping with their problems in an albeit radical and dangerous way, and hiding what they did from everyone around them.

Ginger found the whole experience interesting and helpful, but emotionally draining. The evening had made her realise how many similarities there were between her work and Cameron's, although his patients seemed to vary much more widely in age than did her own. The majority of her patients were teenagers, but

Cameron had people here ranging from seven-teen to forty-two.

She didn't know why she was so surprised, given what she now knew about Cameron, his passion and dedication, but it was eye-opening, watching how great he was with all the members of the group. He seemed to sense by instinct which one needed an arm round the shoulder, which one needed motivation or a challenging goal, who needed to talk, who needed to listen. He gave of himself totally. She couldn't help but be impressed.

When the meeting came to an end, Ginger helped clear the chairs away, then gathered her things together, alarmed to discover that everyone had already dispersed and she was left alone with Cameron. He lounged in the doorway, watching her, and her heart started its usual un-controlled thudding as soon as she looked at him and met the sultry intensity of his gaze.

'I'm glad you were able to join us, Ginger.'

Nodding, she pulled on her coat and hooked the strap of her bag over her shoulder. 'Thank you for asking me. I learned a lot.' Her polite response brought a flicker of a smile to his face.

'Have you eaten?'

'No,' she admitted, surprised by his abrupt change of subject. 'I—'

Taking her hand in his, he led her out of the hall and locked the door. 'There's an excellent Italian restaurant around the corner.'

'Oh, but—'

'Come on, there's lots for us to talk about,' he insisted, cutting off her protests once more.

Cursing herself for her weakness, she walked beside him, all too conscious of the feel of his fingers linked with hers, warm and strong. The evening was overcast and damp after a day of rain, and the breeze was still strong, tossing wayward strands of hair around her face. She was glad when they reached the restaurant, lured inside by the mellow lighting, delicious scents and welcoming warmth, and she sought to regroup and regain her control as Cameron released her hand and they waited to be seated.

'Hello, Dr O'Neill.'

Ginger swung round in surprise at the sound of the soft, feminine voice. 'Jules?' Her eyes widened as she faced the young woman whose brown eyes were shining, and who looked a picture of health and sophistication in her smart suit, her dark hair professionally styled. A broad smile curved Ginger's mouth. 'You look *amazing!* Positively glowing.'

'Thanks. I haven't seen you in a while.' An attractive blush pinkened the twenty-four-year-old's cheeks. 'Are you here for dinner?'

'Yes. This is Dr Kincaid. He works in a similar area to me. Cameron, this is Jules, one of my success stories.'

'Good to meet you, Jules.' He smiled, shaking her hand.

'And you.' She blushed again, juggling the menus she was carrying before holding out her left hand for Ginger to admire the sparkling solitaire diamond on her ring finger. 'I'm getting married next spring.'

Thrilled with the news, and overjoyed at the confident young woman Jules had become, Ginger gave her a hug. 'That's fantastic. Congratulations! Who's the lucky guy?'

'Antonio. His family owns the restaurant,' Jules explained.

'And are you working here, too?'

'Yeah. Can you imagine? Me with all this

food!' She giggled at the irony, happier than Ginger had ever seen her. 'Antonio is the chef, so you can kind of say food is still my life, but in a whole better way!'

Ginger laughed, delighted at the change in Jules. 'It certainly agrees with you.'

'Let me find you a nice table.'

'Thanks, Jules.'

They followed as she led them through the busy restaurant to a secluded table near the rear. Ginger wanted to protest that it was far too intimate, inwardly alarmed at being marooned there with Cameron and all that temptation, but she didn't have the heart to disappoint Jules, who continued to fuss over them.

'She's great.' Cameron smiled as Jules left them to peruse the menu.

'She is.' Ginger watched her go, emotion warming her inside. 'I'm so proud of her. She had a real struggle with bulimia and it took a lot of work to change her relationship with food and raise her self-esteem. This job can be so hard, but it's people like Jules who make it all worthwhile.'

'You should be proud of you, too, you know. What you do for the Juleses of this world is special, Ginger. You're great at what you do—and you care so much.'

'Too much sometimes,' she confessed, glowing from his praise and appreciation.

'The day we stop caring or feeling involved is the day we should pack it in and take up pig breeding or something.'

'Pig breeding?' she challenged on a gurgle of laughter.

He tried to look offended but his grey eyes gleamed with answering amusement. 'It was just an expression. But I'll have you know, I happen to have a soft spot for rare-breed pigs.'

'Oh, ar!' She struggled to put on a thick West Country accent. 'I can just see Farmer Cameron, up to his ears in muck.'

'You can mock, but you'd be surprised what I could turn my hand to.'

Ginger doubted that. Cameron Kincaid was a man of many talents, and she knew all too well how gifted he was with his hands! Fortunately, she was saved from replying—and from her erotic imaginings—when Jules returned to take their order, bringing them a jug of iced water and a basket of delicious home-made rolls, still warm and fragrant.

'So, tell me why you decided to focus your career on eating disorders,' Cameron said once they were alone again, breaking open a roll.

Ginger's humour evaporated and she sat back, frowning as she took a sip of her water. This wasn't something she ever talked about, and yet she found herself opening up to Cameron. 'My older sister, Dee. She had anorexia throughout her early teens. It dominated our home life. My parents didn't know what to do with her and we watched as Dee went from a pretty and intelligent girl to someone suffering this terrible emotional pain. There were daily battles over food, rows, lies, denial, the tricks Dee pulled…' She shook her head at the memories. 'It tore the family apart. First in coping with everything the illness meant, fighting for non-existent help, and then trying to pick up the pieces when Dee died aged seventeen. A wasted life. I vowed then that I would do all I could to help others like her who had no one to turn to, to try and stop them and their families going the same way.'

She didn't realise that Cameron had moved closer until his hand came to rest on her thigh. The warmth and comfort of his touch seeped through her. 'Ginger... I had no idea,' he murmured, his voice rough with understanding.

'No reason why you should.' She fought to control her emotions, not only at the loss of her sister and the destruction of her family life, but the new barriers that remained between herself and her mother. 'Losing Dee, failing her, as he saw it, broke my father's heart. He was never the same man afterwards and he died less than two years later. I was fifteen. After a while my mother re-married, and she and Frank moved to Blackpool where they run a bed and breakfast. She won't talk about Dee at all, and she doesn't take any interest in my work. In fact, she's angry at me. She thinks it was wrong of me to choose this career because it brings back too many memories, too much pain. Sometimes I wonder if maybe she's right.'

'No, you don't. And she's not right.' The pressure of his fingers on her thigh increased, the heat of desire and flare of arousal overtaking the initial sensation of comfort as his hand unconsciously massaged her flesh. 'Don't doubt yourself, Ginger. You've given so much to people. Look at Jules, look at all the others who have needed you and who you have helped.'

She bit her lip, all too aware of the effect his touch was having on her, and she released a shaky sigh of relief when their food arrived and Cameron was forced to remove his hand and shift back into place.

'Don't you ever feel that we barely scratch the surface of what's needed?' she asked, her appetite subdued as she toyed with her pasta.

'All the time.' His smile understanding, he twizzled spaghetti round his fork. 'It's an occupational hazard.'

'Seeing me, or anyone else, for an hour a week, fortnight or month, just isn't enough. Some of these kids need proper intervention, inpatient stays, often for some time. They need re-feeding, they need to be educated about nutrition, they need to regain self-worth and self-esteem. It can't be done overnight or at a distance. Or by people without the proper training and understanding. Some of them aren't even in school because they are ill or bullied or depressed,' Ginger fretted. 'We need more services, not less, more funding, not cut-backs. It's not good enough. And that's why I'm so desperate to get my clinic off the ground. It's a drop in a very big ocean, but I want to do all I can to educate, to give some hope and prospects for the future.'

Cameron frowned as he listened to Ginger speak so passionately about her work. She cared so much. But so did he. She had been through so much personally to reach this point. But so had he. It explained a great deal about her and her drive, and why her dedication matched his own, but it also made things even more complicated when it came to the question of the Ackerman money. One of them was gong to lose out. Big time.

All Ginger had said applied equally to his own self-harm patients and their needs. Neither group was more deserving than the other, there just wasn't the funding to go around, and with more and more demands on the health service, and higher expectations from patients, it meant that there was even less in the budget for the not so well known areas like self-harm and eating disorders. Many other disciplines faced the same problem as money was channelled to front-line services. They were all fighting for scraps from the same table.

Not wanting their rare time alone together to

turn melancholy, or to focus only on work and the conflict that remained unspoken between them, Cameron waited until their plates had been cleared and their glass dishes of Italian ice cream arrived before he edged closer again and attempted to lighten the atmosphere, to steer things towards more personal matters.

'I heard tell that you're a secret adventuress,' he murmured, seeing the surprise in her eyes and the way her face flushed at his words. Was she thinking about their wildly passionate night in London? He certainly was.

'I beg your pardon?'

Her husky voice wrapped around him. Heat flared inside and his gut tightened as she licked a lingering smudge of minty ice cream from succulent lips. It was all he could do not to lean over and perform the task for her himself. 'You indulge in dangerous sports in your rare time off.'

'It helps me unwind, release some of the pressure with a burst of adrenalin,' she admitted after a moment, looking both wary and uncertain.

'Unwinding's good.' And he sure as hell always felt a burst of adrenalin when he was around Ginger. He could think of plenty of ways of releasing some pressure with her, too, but for now he needed to focus on finding out what she was doing this weekend. 'So, you are off on a jaunt tomorrow.'

'How did you know that?'

Cameron set down his spoon and smiled at her. 'A little bird told me.'

'A little bird?' He watched her puzzling it out, a frown knotting her brow. 'Don't tell me. Pip's turned traitor.'

'What can I say? She likes me.'

Ginger didn't respond to his teasing, her frown changing to a scowl. 'I don't appreciate you spying on me.'

'I wasn't spying.' His own humour evaporated. This was not going the way he had hoped. 'Pip didn't break any confidences, we were just chatting over coffee. She's worried about you working so hard, and was relieved you were taking the weekend off.' He reached out and took her hand, resisting her half-hearted attempt to pull away. 'Ginger, I just want to spend some time with you away from work. Is that so bad?'

'It's not bad...I just don't think it's sensible. We should try and keep things professional.'

That old chestnut. 'The way I feel about you isn't remotely professional,' he murmured, dropping his voice, seeing the way her eyes darkened with arousal in response to what she saw in his own. He brushed his thumb across her wrist and felt the rapid beat of her pulse. 'Let me share the weekend with you.'

'You want me to cancel my plans for you?'

'No!' He sighed as her eyes narrowed in disapproval. He really wasn't explaining himself very well. 'I want to come with you—share your adventure.'

An unexpected smile twitched her lips. 'You want to come with me?'

'Absolutely.'

'But you don't even know where I'm going or what I'm doing.'

'I don't care,' he responded recklessly, before a flicker of doubt set in at the mischievous glint in her eye. 'Provided you don't expect me to get stuck in any confined spaces.'

Warmth flushed her cheeks and he knew she was thinking back to the lift in London. 'I wouldn't do that to you.'

'Ginger—'

'Was everything all right with your meal?'

Cameron cursed inwardly as a smiling Jules arrived back at their table and interrupted their conversation. 'Great, thank you.'

'It was lovely, Jules,' Ginger said, freeing her hand from his.

'I told Antonio you were here,' the girl continued, looking over her shoulder with a smile. 'He wants to meet you.' A stocky but attractive young man approached them, his kindly brown eyes full of love when he looked at Jules. 'Toni, this is Dr O'Neill.'

Cameron watched with wry amusement as the Italian grasped Ginger's hands in his and raised them to place a kiss on each. 'How can I ever thank you, Doctor, for all you have done for Jules, for making her well so she can love me?'

'Jules did all the hard work herself.' Ginger smiled at them both with evident affection. 'I'm very proud of her. And delighted that you are both so happy. Congratulations on your engagement.'

'Thank you, thank you. You must come, yes, to the wedding? Both of you?' the ebullient man insisted.

Jules nodded with enthusiasm. 'Please do, Dr O'Neill. We'll send an invitation.'

'That would be very kind,' Ginger allowed gracefully, although Cameron noted that she made no attempt to include him or imply they could be a couple.

Annoyed with himself for being disappointed, Cameron rose to his feet. 'The meal was excellent, thank you. It's time for us to leave, though. I'll come and pay the bill.'

'But no!' Antonio looked horrified. 'No, not at all. No bill. Always, always it is on the house here for you as thanks for all you did for Jules.'

'You don't have to do that,' Ginger protested.

Antonio clasped her hand again, his gaze beseeching. '*Sì*, of course. I want to.'

'Please let us do this for you,' Jules added.

'Well…'

'Thank you, we really appreciate it,' Cameron intervened when Ginger hesitated and looked at him for assistance.

'Just this once, then.' Ginger smiled and hugged Jules again before shaking Antonio's hand. 'It was a lovely evening.'

Cameron helped Ginger on with her coat and took her arm as Jules and Antonio saw them to the door for final goodbyes.

'They have a business to run,' Ginger fretted, glancing back towards the restaurant. 'I feel bad, letting them pay.'

'You made them happy by accepting their gift. They wanted to show how much they appreciate you.'

'But I was only doing my job.'

A laugh escaped him and he shook his head, wrapping his arm around her shoulders and drawing her closer. 'What you do goes way beyond doing a job, Ginger.'

They walked in silence back to the church hall where their cars were parked. Cameron wondered what she was thinking, wondered how to get the conversation back on track again so he could share time with her over the weekend. At least she didn't pull away from him so he had a few moments of holding her close, feeling her soft curves beside him, and he turned his head so he could breathe in a teasing waft of her fruity scent. A few tendrils of silky flyaway blonde hair caressed his face, and he only just managed to prevent himself stopping in the middle of the pavement, turning her and burying his face against her.

When they reached their cars, Cameron took

her hands in his and leaned back against his passenger door, drawing her towards him. 'Well, here we are.'

'Yes.' She looked up at him and he wished he could see more of her expression in the glow the streetlight cast in the darkness. 'I should get home.'

Loath to part from her, he slid his arms around her, locking them at the small of her back. 'I hate having to say good night to you.'

'Cam...' His name escaped on a whisper of breath.

'Mmm?'

Yearning to taste her, to touch her, he couldn't resist any longer. His lips met hers, finding her soft and warm and welcoming. Groaning, he deepened the kiss, hot and urgent as their tongues glided, tangled, explored. Her sweet honey taste mixed with a hint of minty ice cream and made him light-headed. He widened his stance, his palms cupping the lush roundness of her rear as he cradled her hips to his, feeling the tremor run through her at the evidence of his arousal. They were a perfect fit. He wanted her with a hunger he'd never experienced with any other woman. But here wasn't the place. Unfortunately. Before things spiralled out of control—as they always seemed to the moment they touched each other—he reluctantly, and all too slowly, drew the kiss to an end. He cuddled her close, resting his chin on the top of her head as she burrowed against him. It took a while for their breathing to calm, for pulses to slow to normal.

'About tomorrow,' he murmured.

She drew back, her gaze meeting his in the scant light. 'You're serious?'

'Definitely.' His hands framed her face, one thumb tracing the outline of her kiss-swollen mouth. 'I want to spend time with you, Ginger, want to share the things you enjoy.'

He held his breath as she paused, the silence stretching between them, tautening his nerves and tightening his gut as he waited for her answer, desperate for her agreement.

'I'll meet you in the car park outside the hospital at six.'

'I can come?' He searched her gaze, over-whelmed that she had consented. Then the details sank in. 'Six? As in 6:00 a.m.? In the morning?'

She chuckled at the dismay he couldn't hide. 'Too early for you?'

'No, I—'

'I can always go alone.'

'No!' His hold on her tightened again and he scowled at her teasing. He'd do anything, any time, if it meant being with her. 'I'll be there. Are you going to tell me where we're going?'

'Nope. You said you wanted an adventure. I'll surprise you.'

'You always do!' He laughed ruefully. She was amazing.

As she moved to open her car, he was unable to resist stealing one more kiss before letting her go.

Ginger's hands rested on his chest for a moment before she slid behind the wheel. She started the engine and opened the window. 'You need to bring trainers, socks, a long-sleeved top like a fleece—not made of cotton—and swim trunks.'

'Swim trunks?'

'That's right.' He could see her eyes twinkle with amusement in the darkness. 'I'll see you tomorrow.'

Cameron stepped back, watching as her tail-lights disappeared from view, and wondered just what the hell he was letting himself in for.

CHAPTER EIGHT

A YELL of excitement echoed above the roar of turbulent water as the seemingly flimsy boat shot its occupants through the pounding rapids rampaging down the rocky river. Bucked around inside, battling with her paddle, Ginger laughed, feeling the buzz of adrenalin and rush of exhilaration rafting the white water always brought her. From her place near the front, she saw what lay ahead, and hung on as the bow of the rubber boat ploughed into a wall of turbulent water, threatening to frustrate their progress, even to tip them over, before releasing them from its hold, propelling them forward again. Streams of spray stung her cheeks, her heart pounded…she had never felt more alive.

They hit a calm patch, giving all eight members of the team—most of whom had never met until that morning—a few moments to catch their breath before the next run of rapids. Ginger looked round, her gaze clashing with Cameron's. Clad in protective clothing, he was as drenched as the rest of them, but his grin boosted her, his eyes shining with evident enjoyment as he entered into the spirit of the trip, making her doubly glad, despite her initial doubts, that she had shared this adventure with him.

He'd been waiting when she'd arrived at the hospital before the cusp of dawn, and her stomach had turned over at the sight of him, heavy-eyed and tousled, but determined. She had driven up to Perthshire while Cameron had slept most of the way, but she didn't mind. It had left her time to question what on earth she had done, agreeing to spend her day off in his company, to share one of her favourite means of letting off steam. She had to be mad. The journey had also allowed her time to shore up her defences and get herself back in some kind of control again. Or so she'd tried to convince herself. She only had to look at him to come unravelled let alone touch him, or kiss him, or remember what it was like to be with him. It was a constant battle between the raging want and the insurmountable reasons why they couldn't be together.

They had stopped for breakfast before arriving at the outdoor adventure centre but she'd refused to give in when he had tried to cajole her into revealing where they were going. She smiled to herself as she recalled the look of surprise on Cameron's face as he had realised just what they would be doing that day. Surprise and a real charge of excitement, which had shown he was up for the challenge.

Throughout the half-hour training session and safety briefing which had followed them changing into the wetsuits, protective cagoules, buoyancy aids and helmets, Cameron had shown that he was taking to the adventure like the proverbial duck to water, learning the paddle strokes, the positioning, the commands and the emergency procedures with the rest of them. None of it was new to Ginger but she always paid close attention, helping any novices who were unsure about anything.

Coming here never ceased to restore her spirit. She enjoyed many on-the-edge activities, from abseiling to bungee-jumping, but white-water rafting was the best—getting back to the wilds, pitting her wits against the elements, running the river and enjoying the environment, sharing time with like-minded people from all walks of life who loved doing the same things she did. This river was of a lower grade, the rapids less rough than she was used to, but Cameron and others booked on the trip were not as experienced, and she really didn't mind. Being here was enough and all the rivers gave her the buzz.

Cameron's arm slid round her from behind and she couldn't prevent herself leaning back against him, resting her chin on his forearm. 'Thanks for sharing today with me, Ginger. It's fabulous. I wouldn't have missed this for anything.' His breath was warm against her wet, chilled skin.

'I'm glad you're having fun.' And she was glad he was there with her, she admitted to herself, spooked by how much she enjoyed his company, how dangerous it was to like him too much.

'I always have fun with you.'

His arm tightened briefly, his lips lingering on a strip of exposed skin of her neck between her helmet and her cagoule, making her pulse race with a whole different kind of excitement. Then he was releasing her and moving back to his place as their guide called for their attention.

'Look sharp, everyone.'

Gary, a young solicitor from Edinburgh, laughed, giving his friend and colleague who sat alongside Ginger a high-five. 'Here we go again!'

'Yay!'

'Bring it on!'

The excited cries from others in the boat increased Ginger's anticipation as the next rapids came into view. The roar of the water increased until she could hardly hear herself think. She dug in her paddle, hanging on as the raft plunged between rocks. A shower of water hit them and she gasped for breath, revelling in the wild ride as they careered down the run.

All too soon the adventure was over. The time had gone far too quickly. Everyone agreed. The disparate group had bonded during the day's activities and now worked together with a mixture of disappointment and lingering euphoria to get the boat and equipment from the water to prepare for the journey by road back to the outdoor centre.

Ginger took off her helmet and shook out her wet, tangled hair, taken by surprise when

Cameron caught hold of her, all but sweeping her off her feet as he hugged her and planted a stirring kiss on her parted lips.

Laughing, she leaned back to smile at him. He looked amazing, dark hair slicked back, his masculine frame filling out the wetsuit in a way that should be illegal. 'What was that for?' Her question was breathless, her emotions stoked from both the last couple of hours running rapids and from Cameron's nearness. It was all too easy, away from work, to forget all the reasons she shouldn't get more attached to him.

'Does there have to be a reason?' Grey eyes, darkened with the fire of enthusiasm mixed with desire, stared into her own, heating her right through. 'It could be a thank-you for a memorable adventure.' His arms tightened, the length of his body pressing against hers. 'It could just be because I can't keep my hands off you and need to kiss you.'

The heat inside her flared into a raging inferno. 'Cameron—'

'Gary! No!'

The cry of alarm and commotion cut off Ginger's words. She looked round, shocked to see that the young solicitor from Edinburgh, who had been clowning around, trying to impress a couple of girls, had fallen. He lay worryingly still, partially in the water. Cameron moved first, releasing her and running towards the casualty. Ginger was hot on his heels.

'What happened?' Cameron demanded, kneeling down beside the prone young man.

'He was joking around and slipped on the rocks.' Shaken, his friend was pale and scared. 'He hit his head.'

Semi-conscious, Gary was drowsy and disorientated, his words slurred and confused. There was blood oozing profusely from the scalp laceration at the back of his head. Concerned, recognising the signs of a likely fracture and the possibility of a serious head injury, Cameron turned to the guide, who had rushed to the scene with the first-aid kit.

'You're a doctor?' the guide queried.

'Yes. I used to be in trauma. How long will it take an ambulance to get out here?' Cameron frowned in dissatisfaction at the response time suggested. 'We're going to need the air ambulance to take Gary to the nearest neurosurgical unit.'

As the guide moved off to place the emergency call, Ginger knelt down opposite him. 'Is it bad?'

'I'm worried. He likely has a compound depressed fracture and his level of consciousness is deteriorating.'

'It's a long time since I had to do any hands-on medical work, but what can I do to help you?'

He glanced up to smile at her, relieved she was there, calm and reassuring. 'We need to stop the bleeding and get him out of the water. He's cold—and I'm concerned about shock. This first-aid kit is good but it just doesn't have the things I need for a situation like this.'

They planned the best and safest way to move Gary to a better position, Ginger taking charge of keeping his head still while Cameron monitored his condition with the limited supplies available.

'Gary, can you hear me?' Cameron shook his head at the drowsy mumble that followed his question, concerned that the young man was slipping further towards unconsciousness. 'Stay with me, Gary.'

Making sure the casualty was positioned with his head slightly raised to reduce the intracranial pressure he was coming to fear, Cameron wished time would pass more quickly and specialist help would arrive. With Ginger's assistance, he had managed to get the bleeding under control and lightly cover the open wound, but he could do little more than monitor and try to stabilise Gary's condition. A CT scan was needed as soon as possible, with surgical intervention to decompress the brain injury, debride and clear any bone fragments that had entered the intracranial cavity and possibly punctured the dura matter, exposing the brain surface. Infection was a risk, as was haematoma and permanent damage. He tried not to look on the gloomy side—difficult with Gary's BP dropping and his other vital signs unpromising as he lapsed further into unconsciousness.

The guide had been a help, keeping the other members of the group out of the way and calm, relaying messages to his base and interacting with the emergency services. Again Cameron met Ginger's gaze, seeing her concern but also her understanding and unspoken support. They had worked well together in a situation that was much more alien to her than to him, although it had been some time since he had worked in a hospital trauma unit. Attending a patient as an emergency out in the wilds was a different matter entirely. But they had coped. So far. If only that help would arrive. The sooner they transferred Gary to a specialist unit, the better the young man's chances of survival and recovery.

A road ambulance was the first to reach them. The paramedics had more specialist equipment, and were able to be in radio contact with the nearest neurosurgical unit, which was giving advice as to what drugs and fluids to administer. Gary was soon intubated and was almost ready for transfer when the air ambulance was heard. They all breathed a huge sigh of relief when it landed as close to them as it could, a trauma doctor on board. Cameron was thankful to hand over the patient, giving the attending physician a full report on what had happened, what had been done and how much Gary had deteriorated.

'You OK?' Ginger asked, moving up beside him as they watched the air ambulance take off to transport their casualty to the nearest neuro-surgical department.

'I'm fine.' He slipped an arm around her shoulders. 'Thanks for your help, you were great.'

'I'm not sure I was that much use, I'm very

rusty. You were impressive, though. I had no idea you'd done trauma work,' she added after a pause, evident curiosity in her voice.

This was neither the time nor the place to tell her about the change in his career—or the reason for it. The thoughts caused a familiar spear of pain to lance his gut. 'It's a long story for another day. For now I just hope Gary makes it.'

'He has a vastly better chance, thanks to you, Cam.' Her reassurance eased some of his doubts. 'No one could have done more.'

'Fingers crossed it was enough.'

Her smile gentle, she took his hand and they walked back to the waiting vehicle. 'Come on, let's go home.'

Once back at the outdoor centre, they parted ways to shower and change into their own clothes. A short while later, Cameron met Ginger outside the main door, finding her talking to Craig, one of the owners of the adventure outfit. The man smiled at him and shook his hand.

'I'm sorry your outing ended as it did, but we are very lucky you were here and thankful for all you did, Dr Kincaid.'

'Cameron.' He smiled back. 'I was glad to help. Hopefully Gary will recover.'

Craig nodded, his expression grave. 'I was telling Ginger that you must both come back and have another rafting trip on us.'

'You don't have to do that. Today was my first experience of white-water rafting, but I'm determined it won't be my last. I had a great time,' Cameron assured him.

'That's good to know! And Ginger is one of our most enthusiastic, if infrequent, visitors.'

Cameron met her gaze, sure she would be there every day if circumstances permitted. Not that he blamed her. They took their leave, both of them content to keep off contentious subjects, instead enthusing over the good side of the day during the first part of their journey home. After a while the silences in the car grew longer, a growing tension and awareness making the small space seem oppressive, charged. Cameron was glad when Ginger switched on the radio, the soothing classical music negating the need for small-talk.

He dozed, thinking of the day…thinking of Ginger. Aside from the emergency at the end, this trip had been just what he had needed. The rafting had been a huge surprise, and he had meant what he'd said, he definitely wanted to do it again—often, if possible. That Ginger shared his love of the outdoors and had such an adventurous nature were more boxes ticked in her favour, more examples of how good they were together. There were rather too many of them for his peace of mind. She was becoming all too important to his very existence and, given what seemed to be an insurmountable conflict between them professionally, he knew he was stepping on dangerous ground, opening himself to heartache if he pursued a personal relationship with her.

Dusk was falling by the time they arrived back in Strathlochan, the hospital silhouetted above the town as the sun dipped behind the hill. Ginger parked her car next to his and switched off the engine. He unclipped his seat belt, but couldn't bring himself to move, to leave her, not wanting their time together to end. Telling himself he was all kinds of fool, that he should walk away and not create more problems for either of them, he nevertheless ignored his head and followed his heart. Taking her hand in his, he turned it over, tracing her palm, stroking her fingers, feeling a tremor ripple through her, even as fire licked through him at the feel of her soft skin against his own.

'Come home with me, Ginger,' he tempted, raising her hand so he could whisper his lips across her wrist, noting the hurried beat of her pulse.

'I shouldn't.'

'You should.'

'Cam…'

He knew she was weakening and ruthlessly pressed his advantage. 'Please. The day doesn't have to end here.'

'But we can't forget—'

'We can,' he refuted urgently, desperate to persuade her they could keep professional and personal separate. He teased circles on her palm with the tip of his tongue. 'We can forget all about everything but us. I want to be with you. I need to make love with you.'

Ginger shivered at the blatant sexuality in Cameron's husky voice. Heat curled through her at his touch and she knew her defences were crumbling. She couldn't deny that she needed him, too. But it was crazy. In the dim light of the car their gazes met. He set her hand down on his jeans-clad thigh, his own covering hers, and she swallowed, feeling the firmness of muscle, the heat of him through the denim fabric. She shouldn't be doing this. She knew she would regret it, that it was wrong for both of them, but right at this moment the terrible ache of want was outweighing her doubts and her common sense.

Without further words, Cameron left her car to return to his own, and within moments she was following him out of the car park, down the hill and through the town, before winding along country lanes, their headlights glinting off tall hedgerows and the trunks of trees. She should stop, turn round, go back. But she didn't. She was a fool, but she was in too deep now, wanted him so frantically that the rational part of her was overcome. It was impetuous, reckless, beyond reason. She knew it, but still she continued to follow his taillights down the darkened lanes.

How could she need him with such desperation when they were going to hurt each other? Maybe it was because they both still yearned for what they had been unable to finish in London. Maybe one more night would finally get this incessant craving out of their systems. It had to, she lectured herself, even while a part of her recognised the futility of her thoughts. Because there could only be one inevitable ending. Either Cameron was going to trample on her dreams and deny the patients she cared about the services they needed to survive, or she was going to do the same to him. And if they were any more involved with each other on a personal level, it would be so much more painful. Oh, help. Her hands tightened on the steering-wheel. She should find the strength to say no to this madness.

Before she could talk herself out of what she was doing, she turned into the driveway of his cottage and parked behind his car. An outside security light came on, illuminating the front of the building. She had a glimpse of an attractive stone-built house under a slate roof, then Cameron was opening her door and holding out his hand, as if scared she would change her mind. She knew she should. Knew she ought to run. Her heart beat crazily in her chest and she felt breathless as she gathered up her bag and placed her free hand in his, allowing him to lead her towards the front door.

Once inside, she scarcely noticed anything about the interior of Cameron's home because she couldn't drag her gaze from his. He switched on a light in the hall and locked the door, then hung up his leather jacket before solicitously helping her set her things on a nearby table and taking her coat. Ginger swallowed, every cell of her body tingling with anticipation.

'Can I get you something to eat?'

Cameron's question permeated the haze of desire in her brain. She shook her head, unable to think about food at a time like this. 'No. Thank you. I'm not hungry.'

'I am. Very hungry.' The low rumble of his voice and the heat darkening his eyes left her in no doubt that he wasn't thinking about food, either. She shivered as he raised a hand, his fingers brushing her face, trailing along her neck and lingering at the pulse point of her throat. The fevered ache inside her intensified. 'You make me ravenous.'

She could hear every erratic beat of her heart as he took her hand again and led her up the stairs. They walked along the corridor, every footstep raising her pulse rate and her expectations, her fingers clinging to his as he drew her into his bedroom. He switched on a pair of bedside lights, casting a muted glow throughout the room. Her gaze skimmed over the large, inviting bed before clashing with his again. She couldn't help but remember London. That magical night when they had done pretty much everything with each other but the one thing they had both wanted...knowing each other in the fullest sense of the word. Now she was both excited and nervous.

'Ginger...'

She heard an edge in his voice and frowned, concerned at the look on his face. 'What's the matter?'

'I should tell you I haven't been to the chemist.'

'No!' She stared at him in horrified disappointment and took a few steps backwards.

'I'm sorry.'

Ginger wanted to cry. This couldn't be happening to them again. Then she saw his lips twitch and her eyes narrowed in suspicion. 'Cameron?'

'Yes, Ginger?'

'If you're teasing me, I'm going to kill you.'

'Yeah?' A chuckle rumbled in his chest. 'You and whose army?'

She put her hands on his midriff, intending to push him back on the bed, but he caught her wrists, pulling her down with him, then rolling so she was under him. Her breath caught as he moved so her hips cradled his, and she could feel his arousal through the barrier of their clothes. She whimpered, trying unsuccessfully to free her hands, needing to touch him, wanting nothing between them. But he held her captive, his mouth taking hers in a searing, consuming, possessive kiss that instantly reignited the dangerous passion and engulfed her in flames once more. He moved against her, simulating what they both most wanted, and she arched her body to his in needy frustration.

Cameron dragged his mouth from hers and she gasped, sucking air into starved lungs as he nibbled a path down her throat. 'Cam, please…'

'You drive me insane.' His voice was a throaty growl against her skin, his words stripping her of any remaining shred of control. 'I want to devour you.'

Releasing her hands, his fingers began to undo the buttons down the front of her shirt, spreading the fabric aside, feasting his appreciative gaze on her. Her fingers sank into his hair as bent his head, kissing his way over her stomach, making her shiver and her muscles tighten. Lifting his head, he watched her as he traced his fingers round the edge of the lacy tops of her bra cups. She could feel her hardened nipples pushing against the restraining fabric. His thumbs rubbed over them and she bit her lip to keep from crying out at the sensation, wanting to feel his mouth there. Sliding his hands under her, he deftly slipped the clasp free, then he was brushing the fabric aside, exposing her to his gaze. His hands covered her, shaping sensually, making her gasp as he rolled one proud peak between finger and thumb before he bent his head again, taking the needy flesh into his mouth to torment it with teeth and tongue. When she thought she couldn't stand the exquisite torture another moment, he drew her into his mouth, suckling strongly. Ginger arched up, thinking she would die from the pleasure of it, blindly wrestling with his jumper, desperate to feel his skin against her own.

He helped her, tossing the garment aside before turning his attention to her skirt, swiftly removing it, then easing her panties down her legs and dropping them off the bed. As her own fingers fumbled with the fastening of his jeans, he ignored her protest, moving away to stand by the bed. She watched as he stripped off his remaining clothes, leaving her breathless all over again as she looked at the perfection of his body. A very aroused body.

'Please, tell me you were joking,' she whispered hoarsely, clenching her hands to fists to prevent herself reaching for him. 'Please, tell me you have something.'

'Would I let you down?'

A wicked smile curved his mouth as he opened one of the drawers in the nightstand and took out a large bag. Her eyes widened as he tipped it up and an array of assorted condom boxes scattered over the duvet.

'Cam, you're outrageous!'

'The job has its perks. I stocked up on some samples, just in case.' He smiled, kneeling on the bed as he sorted through the packets. 'What do you fancy? Flavoured? R—?'

Ginger sat up and put her hand over his mouth, cutting off the naughty flow of words. She saw the dark fire of passion in his compelling grey eyes as she grazed her hands over the muscled contours of his hair-brushed chest. 'You. I just fancy you.'

'Damn, Ginger. I have no control around you.' He groaned, taking her back down on the bed, his fingers setting out on a tantalising exploration which took her breath away.

The texture of his skin under her own roving hands excited her, his earthy male aroma stirred her senses, and she opened her mouth on his shoulder, tasting him, biting at him, wanting him to hurry.

'I want to love you for hours.' His voice was shaky with needy impatience. 'But I don't think I can wait.'

She dragged her nails down his spine, delighting in the tremor that ran through him. 'I don't want you to wait. I need you inside me.'

Eyes nearly black with passion, he looked down at her for a long moment, his breathing ragged. Her whole body felt as if it was going to explode if she didn't know what it was like to be joined with him. Now.

'Please, Cam,' she begged, writhing helplessly against him.

'Will you still respect me in the morning?'

She laughed at his teasing, at the same time cursing him for wasting time. 'Not if you don't hurry up!'

He reached out, and she saw his fingers were unsteady as he opened one of the boxes. Foil ripped, and she took the protection from him, smiling at his indrawn hiss of breath as she took her time sheathing him, her fingers lingering to stroke and explore.

'Enough.'

His hands journeyed over her body…her breasts, her stomach, between her thighs, making her moan as he stroked her intimately.

'Cam,' she gasped.

'No more waiting,' he promised, giving her a deep, hard kiss. He moved to her and she pulled him closer, biting her lip against her cry when she felt him there, at last. 'Open your eyes, Ginger. I want to watch you as I fill you.'

Scarcely able to breathe, her heated gaze locked with his as she wrapped her legs around him, her nails digging into his back as he united them with one sure, heavy movement. Her body felt impossibly, exquisitely possessed, as if they had been made for each other, a perfect fit. It was blissful. Magnificent. She never wanted it to end.

'Oh, God, Cam.'

'Finally.' He groaned, and the look of intense sexuality and pleasure on his face made her nearly lose it right away. 'You feel so good.'

'Please...' She whimpered as he buried his face in her neck, his stubble rasping against her sensitised skin. Impatient, her breath ragged, every fibre of her being on fire, she arched to him, desperate for him to move. 'Please. Don't stop.'

One hand fisted in her hair and he raised his head, his gaze frenzied with passionate intent as he looked at her. 'I'm never stopping. Never,' he vowed roughly.

His control broken, he slid one arm under her hips, keeping her with him, and she tightened her grip, urging him on. She could do no more than hold on for the ride as he took her on a wildly sensual and erotic journey. Ginger wasn't sure she would survive it. She had wondered what this would be like, had known from their time in London that Cameron was a supremely generous lover, giving and considerate, deeply passionate, excitingly rough yet gentle, too, but she had never before experienced such earth-shattering pleasure, such a tumult of sensation and emotion. She felt abandoned, uninhibited, wild.

'Yes, yes. Please,' she encouraged, her cries growing increasingly loud as he took her from one incredible pinnacle of pleasure to another.

When he finally pushed her over the edge to a shuddering, amazing climax, one that never seemed to end, she clung to him, scared she would faint from the magnitude of it, plunging into an abyss of searing sensation from which she had no idea if she would ever return. Cameron groaned as her body spasmed around him, and he took his own release, calling her name, spiralling with her into the raging vortex of pleasure. As he continued to drive into her, her hands encouraged him, his rough cry of release exciting her, giving her a unique sense of feminine power.

'Dear God.' He collapsed against her, taking a few moments before shifting his weight from her, wrapping his arms around her and holding her close. His heart pounded as madly as hers, and they both struggled for breath, their bodies trembling. 'Ginger…'

She had no energy to speak, either, no energy to do anything except rest exhausted but deliciously sated in his arms. They dozed, she didn't know for how long, but when she woke up, moonlight cast a silvery glow through the room. Stretching naked on the bed, she suddenly realised Cam was watching her. She smiled, sighing as he shifted, his hands and mouth beginning a new exploration, his gaze assessing her reaction to his every slow, thorough caress, devoting himself to bringing her endless pleasure.

Ginger had no idea how many times they reached for each other in the night. They certainly didn't get much sleep. Sometimes their loving was fast and urgent, sometimes tantalisingly slow and tender. She felt cherished, and she gave Cam as much attention as he gave her. It was perfect. They were so attuned to one another. The sex was incredible, but so was the closeness they shared, the companionship, the humour between them, the intimacy—and that scared the hell out of her.

It wasn't meant to be like this. Even knowing they had no future, she had allowed herself to get too close, too involved. It was as if they were two halves of a whole, but nothing could change the circumstances of their working lives, which put them on opposite sides of an impossible divide. If it was just herself who would be affected, she could live with it, take the chance and explore where this attraction could go. But hers was not a job she could leave without causing upheaval to others. So many people, who had no one else, depended on her.

She had made a monumental mistake. Selfishly she had taken this night with Cameron, giving in to the impossible passion that pulled them together. Whatever happened now, they were both going to be hurt. Tears stung her eyes as she looked at his sleeping form, her fingers softly brushing a few strands of hair back from his forehead. She didn't want to cause him pain. The kind of pain that was crushing her insides now because she had known this was wrong and yet she had still done it, had given in to her own needs without considering the consequences. For both of them.

Stifling a sob, she slipped silently from the bed and gathered up her clothes. It was time to leave. Now. Before things became any more complicated. Not that they could. For her, at least. Because she had committed the most un-forgivable sin of all. Against all her better judge-ment and common sense, she had fallen in love with Cameron Kincaid, the one man she could never have, the man whose professional dreams she might destroy...or who might destroy hers.

CHAPTER NINE

'Pip, can I have a word?'

The matronly nurse turned from escorting a worryingly thin young girl across to the outpatient registration desk. 'One minute, Cameron, and I'll be with you. I just have to help Tess with something.' Pip smiled, her hazel eyes kind and understanding.

Nodding, Cameron waited with mounting impatience. Anger, hurt, disappointment, fear. He wasn't sure which of the emotions burning inside him was the strongest, but they had all eaten away at him since he had woken up on Sunday morning to find himself alone. He hadn't thought the night in London with Ginger could be improved on, but Saturday had surpassed it to an unbelievable degree. And she had run from him. Again. To say he was ticked off was an under-statement. Damn her! How could she switch her feelings, her passion, on and off like that? Did it really not matter to her at all? Had it just been sex? Granted, it had been the most incredible sex he'd ever experienced, but for him it was so much more than just the physical. He wanted Ginger. All of her. Heart, body and soul. And given how commitment and relationship phobic he was, even admitting that to himself scared the hell out of him.

He'd had plans for Sunday. A whole day loving her, getting to know more about her. He had even decided to confide in her about Molly so she would understand his own motivations, his need to do what he did. But Ginger had rejected him once more. It hurt more than he thought possible. He wanted to rail at her, curse the injustice of it, demand some answers, but he was scared that if he pushed too hard he would drive her away completely. Somehow he had to curb his impatience and do all he could to woo her back onside, to ensure he stayed close to her, to persuade her again that, despite the fact they were competing for the Ackerman money, what they had together was too special to throw away. There had to be a way to make things work—yet he was filled with doubt, scared he was going to lose her.

Attempts to contact Ginger at home and the hospital had proved unfruitful and his own appointments had kept him busy all Monday morning. Now it was approaching lunchtime and this was the first opportunity he'd had to collar Pip and seek some assistance and some answers. His gaze strayed around the outpatient seating area where several people were waiting to be called for their various appointments and consultations. A harassed-looking middle-aged woman was having difficulty controlling a couple of unruly boys who were running around annoying other people, especially the large young lady who looked stricken and as if she was about to flee at any moment. Her hands nervously shredded a tissue, and her eyes, on the rare occasions she glanced up, were awash with misery and the threat of tears. He wondered why she was there and why she was so scared.

'Cameron, how are you?' Pip reclaimed his attention, her shrewd gaze assessing as she observed him. 'You look as edgy and unhappy as Ginger is today.'

He sucked in a breath. 'Is she nearly finished with her appointments? I need to talk to her and she's avoiding me. Again.'

'I'm sorry, but she's still busy. Our clinic is running late this morning,' Pip explained, placing a hand on his arm as if she understood his frustration. 'A common occurrence. Ginger always gives each patient the time they need, which means we're usually behind schedule.'

The news didn't surprise him. He knew how caring and conscientious Ginger was. But he only had a short time for a break himself as he had commitments of his own to fulfil and he couldn't wait around much longer in the hope of catching Ginger alone.

'Tell me, Cameron, have you thought what you'll do if you don't win this man's donation?'

Pip's question caught him unawares and he frowned at her in surprise. 'Not really. I'll continue with all the work I have but try elsewhere to gain support for the clinic and do all I can to make it happen. I certainly won't give up.'

'Your work means a great deal to you?'

'Yes. It does.'

'Does Ginger know why?' Pip asked. 'Have

you explained to her why you feel as deeply as she does about your patients and your intentions for your own clinic?'

Cameron shook his head. 'Not yet. It's one of the things I want to talk about with her.'

Pip paused a moment and regarded him thoughtfully. 'Did you know that our department is closing next spring?'

'No! I had no idea. I thought…' He broke off. What had he thought? That Ginger would just go on here at the hospital if her own plans for her unit didn't materialise?

'We've already been told our funding is to be cut and our work absorbed into the general psychological service. There'll be no place for Ginger in Strathlochan,' Pip continued, bringing a cold knot of dread to his stomach. 'Not that she cares about herself. She'll be snapped up by any eating disorders centre. What is eating her up is the thought of what will happen to the patients here without specialist care. She feels she will be letting them down.'

Which brought them back to the crux of the whole problem, he realised. 'I can't let my patients down, either, Pip, or my other backers.

I can't step aside and not try for the Ackerman money.' Cursing, he ran the fingers of one hand through his hair.

'I'm not suggesting that you do, lovey. You have your own responsibilities and that is as it should be.'

'So what are you saying?'

Pip's hand squeezed his. 'Try to understand how difficult this is for her. Ginger's scared, Cameron. She's always put her work before herself, she has never been interested in anyone before, has never needed to consider that a balance may be possible. Her heart is torn between her very real duty, her need to do her job, and her fear that all this is ultimately going to hurt you both if you get more involved. Give her some time—but don't give up on her.'

It might not be what he had wanted to hear, but it was good advice. Sighing, he managed a smile and bent to kiss Pip's cheek. 'Thanks.'

'No problem. Now, I must get back to work.'

Cameron watched her go, his thoughts in turmoil, undecided what he should do next about Ginger. Once again his attention was distracted by a new commotion in the waiting area. One of the young boys was running in and out of the chairs. He skidded round a corner, crashing in to the large girl who had tried to cower in a corner out of the way.

'Fat cow, you take up too much room,' the boy said loudly and abusively.

Angry, seeing the embarrassment and dismay on the girl's face, Cameron walked across, catching hold of the hood of the boy's top and gently bringing him to a halt. 'This is a hospital, not a playroom, and there's no excuse to be rude,' he rebuked quietly but firmly, leading the boy back to his stressed mother.

'I'm so sorry.' She looked up at him and he noted the dark circles under her lifeless brown eyes. 'It won't happen again.'

He smiled with sympathy. 'They must be a handful.'

'That's one way of putting it,' she agreed, managing a ghost of a smile in return.

Concerned, Cameron walked across to where the young woman sat. He guessed she was in her early twenties, and she had platinum-blonde hair and a pale complexion. She was also visibly shaking. 'Hi,' he greeted her, waiting a few steps away so as not to crowd her. Finally, she looked up at him with dove-grey eyes bruised with fear and hurt.

'H-hi,' she stammered in response, looking stunned that he had spoken to her.

'Do you mind if I sit down?' Renewed surprise and wariness flared in her eyes before she gave a hesitant nod. Aching for her, Cameron seated himself beside her. 'Are you all right?'

'Yes. Fine.'

The response was polite but he didn't believe her. She seemed almost paralysed with fear. 'I'm Cameron Kincaid. What's your name?'

'L-Louise. Louise K-Kerr.'

'Good to meet you, Louise.' He glanced at her and saw the way she stared down at the floor, a flush stripping the paleness from her cheeks. 'Are you waiting to see someone?'

'I'm m-meant to be. B-But I think I'd b-better go h-home.'

'That would be a shame...now you've taken the big step and come here.' He praised her sincerely, knowing how intimidating hospitals could be and how frightened some people were of facing the unknown. Louise's case was extreme, though. 'Who is your appointment with?'

'Dr O'Neill.'

His heart lurched at the mention of the name but he didn't know why he was so surprised that Louise should be one of Ginger's patients. He was also relieved. There would be no one better than Ginger to tread softly and be gentle with Louise's feelings. 'I think you should stay.'

'Do you kn-know her?' Louise asked after a moment, her voice soft and uncertain.

'I do.' And how! He forced away X-rated memories of their amazing night together. 'Have you not met her before?'

Louise shook her head. 'This is my first time here. I—I don't like doctors. Except my new GP. She's been wonderful. I'm only here because she persuaded me it would help.'

'I'm sure it will,' Cameron reassured her. 'Ginger's lovely, Louise. I can promise you that you won't be sorry if you see her.'

Wide, anxious eyes looked at him. 'Really?'

'Really. There's no one better.'

Cameron thought of Jules, the young woman he'd met at the Italian restaurant on Friday night, and the transformation that had clearly occurred in her life. Louise's self-esteem appeared non-existent. He had no idea what her story was, but he would bet that a few months of Ginger's care would find her brimming with new-found confidence. It made him proud, knowing what a special doctor Ginger was, but it also made him mad that her patients were to be denied her care with the funding cut, and uneasy what would happen once the news came through about the Ackerman money.

He snapped off his thoughts, a rush of desire sending heat searing through him as Ginger came through the swing doors from the direction of the consulting rooms and led a teenage boy across to a worried-looking couple who rose to greet them.

Giving Louise a friendly nudge, he pointed across the waiting area. 'There's Ginger now.'

'That's Dr O'Neill?'

Cameron smiled at the surprise in Louise's voice, hoping Ginger's lush curves and sexy femininity would give the young woman confidence she wouldn't be judged but would be treated with respect and understanding. Dressed in a floaty, colourful skirt and loose shirt, her sunshine-blonde hair left loose, Ginger didn't look like a stereotypical doctor. When Ginger shook hands with the couple and waved them goodbye, she turned to survey the room and called Louise's name. He knew the moment Ginger saw him, registered her awareness, the mix of alarm and desire in her turquoise eyes, the hesitation in her step as she crossed to join them.

'Hello, Ginger.' It was a struggle, but he kept everything professional and resisted the urgent temptation to touch her, kiss her, carry her off to his cave. 'This is Louise. We were just having a chat.'

Her smile warm and genuine, she shook the young woman's hand. 'Great. Hi, Louise, it's lovely to meet you. I'm so sorry I've kept you waiting.'

'Th-That's OK.'

Cameron met Ginger's gaze as Louise nervously gathered up her coat and bag. He saw the question in her eyes as she mouthed, 'Problem?'

With an imperceptible nod, he glanced at Louise, making sure she was otherwise occupied before silently mouthing back, 'She's scared.'

Ginger seemed unsurprised at the information and he smiled, having complete confidence that

Louise would be cared for and was now in the best of hands with Ginger on her side.

Louise rose to her feet and looked at him with a shaky smile, a shy blush on her face. 'Thank you for sitting with me.'

'No problem. Trust me, you'll be fine with Dr O'Neill.'

He watched as Ginger slid a reassuring arm around Louise and guided her through the door and along the corridor to her room. It was clear to him that he wasn't going to have any opportunity to talk to Ginger now. Restless and frustrated, he headed to the canteen for a hasty lunch before his afternoon appointments caught up with him, wondering when he was going to next get her alone...and how they were going to reconcile the conflict that was still keeping them apart.

'Dr Kate Anderson.'

'Hello, Kate, it's Ginger O'Neill from Strathlochan. I'm sorry I didn't phone you sooner but yesterday was manic,' she explained to the GP from Glentown-on-Firth, who had referred Louise Kerr to her.

It was early on Tuesday morning and Ginger

fought down waves of tiredness. She had been at her desk for a while, ploughing through her pile of paperwork to try to catch up before she went downstairs to begin the day's appointments.

'I confess I've been in suspense,' Kate admitted with a wry laugh. 'Tell me, did Louise keep her appointment?'

Talking about the young woman she had met for the first time the day before made Ginger think of Cameron, too. 'She did. But I gather it was a close thing. Louise was very scared and on the point of bolting when one of my colleagues from a different specialty took her under his wing and persuaded her to stay. He waited with her until I was free.'

'Goodness. Louise doesn't give her trust easily.' Kate's surprise was obvious. 'Please, thank him for me.'

'I will.'

Ginger grimaced at her promise. Cameron had been wonderful with Louise. She knew she had to thank him, too, for his insightful compassion—a difficult task when she had been trying to avoid him since her cowardly exit from his home on Sunday morning.

'And thank you, Ginger. As I told you when we first spoke when I referred her, Louise has had such a rotten time of it with the medical profession in the past and it has taken eighteen months for her to feel comfortable with me,' the caring GP explained. 'We've slowly begun to sort out some of her health problems but it's been a struggle for me to encourage her to tackle her emotional issues. Do you think you can help her?'

'It will take a while for her to feel at ease here, but we had a good talk yesterday, and if she keeps coming to see me, I'm confident we can work well together.'

'That's excellent news!'

Ginger glanced down at the file and her own initial notes. 'Louise is clearly very shy and lacking in self-worth. We only touched on some of her issues yesterday, but she appears to have coped with her bad experiences and emotional problems by turning to food. That's not uncommon. She told me she's yo-yo'd wildly with her weight for many years and has spells where she binges or eats compulsively. In my experience it can be a way of self-comfort or self-punishment—sometimes both.'

'That makes sense,' Kate agreed thoughtfully. 'I know she has had problems at home, school and work. There was a lot of bullying, a lot of verbal and emotional abuse. Now she finds it hard to make friends, to let people close to her, because she's been let down and hurt so many times.'

'It will take time, Kate, but I'm confident we can make a difference. Louise is going to come here to see me and my team once a month, but I'm going to keep in touch with her by telephone between appointments, at least initially, so she gets used to me and has the confidence to come back. I'll keep you updated as we go along,' she promised, making a note in her diary.

'I really appreciate it,' Kate responded with relief, and Ginger could tell that the family doctor had taken Louise's case to her heart. 'Conor said you were good.'

Ginger smiled with affection as she thought of Kate's husband and fellow GP. Their marriage just over a year ago had taken one of south-west Scotland's most eligible and popular bachelors out of commission. 'How is the old rogue?'

'He's a totally besotted daddy! At five months

old, Rebecca already has him wrapped round her little finger.' Kate laughed.

After her talk with Kate, Ginger reviewed her cases for the day. She was sipping her umpteenth cup of coffee when Pip arrived in her office, patient notes in her hand.

'Morning, Ginger.' She sat down, a concerned frown on her face. 'You're looking tired, lovey.'

'Mmm. We seem to be busier than ever at the moment. I've had several more referrals, but how we are going to fit any more new patients into an already overstretched schedule, I have no idea.'

Pip nodded sympathetically. 'Not that you'll ever turn anyone away.'

'I can't, Pip.' She finished her coffee and sat back with a sigh. 'How the powers that be can think of closing this department when the patient need is so obvious defeats me.'

'I know. It's not right.'

Their conversation was interrupted when her assistant buzzed her from the outer office. 'Yes, Sarah?'

'The dishy Dr Kincaid is on the phone for you.'

Ginger felt a blush heat her face at Pip's knowing smile. 'What does he want?'

'He says it's about a patient,' Sarah replied.

She really didn't want to talk with him, it was too awkward given what had gone between them, and how she still felt every time she so much as thought of him. But… 'OK, Sarah. Put him through.' She cursed her foolish weakness.

'Hi, Ginger. How are you?'

'I'm fine.' If she didn't count the way she nearly melted just at the sound of his voice.

'I can't stop thinking about you.'

She bit her lip as need slammed through her. Uncomfortable talking with him in front of Pip, her manner was stilted. 'I'm in a meeting. Sarah said you wanted to talk about a patient.'

'Yes.' He sighed, his disappointment evident, but he was nothing but professional when he spoke again. 'I was called in urgently to a young woman who is believed to have been cutting and burning herself. Turns out you've seen her before for bulimia. Angela Strachan.'

'Damn. I remember her.'

'I know you're busy but can you come down to Casualty?'

Ginger considered the request. She couldn't allow her awareness of and need to avoid

Cameron personally to affect the welfare of a patient, but that didn't mean it was going to be easy having to see or work with him. 'I have a heavy case-load of appointments but I'll look out her notes and come to Casualty first.'

'Thanks, Ginger. See you soon.'

She hung up and filled Pip in on developments, trying to ignore the way her insides churned just at the thought of the man. After printing out a summary on Angela Strachan, she gathered up the files she needed for her morning appointments, then had a quick word with Sarah. Once free, she headed downstairs with Pip, leaving her paperwork in her consulting room and arranging for Pip to make a start on their clinic.

'Don't worry,' her colleague reassured her, ever calm and understanding. 'We'll manage, we always do.'

'I'll be back as soon as I can.'

'Ginger?'

Hearing the edge in Pip's voice, she reluctantly turned at the door. 'Yes?'

'I know you find it difficult to switch off and separate your work from your own needs, but give Cameron a chance,' the older woman advised. 'The sexual chemistry between you is amazing...the windows fog whenever you're together for even five seconds!'

'Pip—'

'I know, it isn't my business, and you're worried what will happen about the patients when the decision comes in about the funding. But things can be worked out, lovey, if you want it badly enough. You deserve your own happiness and Cameron is special. Now, I've said my piece. You get off and I'll set to work,' she said briskly, a smile in her kind hazel eyes.

Ginger tried to put her feelings for Cameron and her confusion about the conflict between them to one side in order to focus on Angela Strachan's needs. As she went into the busy A and E department, the first person she saw was Dr Will Brown, renowned for his blond good looks and irrepressible humour.

'Hello, gorgeous,' he greeted her with a cheeky smile.

'Hi, Will. How are you?'

'Great.' He tucked a chart under his arm and drew her aside to make way for a nurse who was wheeling an injured patient up to Radiology. 'We haven't seen you here for a while.'

Aside from Danielle Watson's emergency admission, Ginger was thankful she hadn't needed to be called for some time. 'I was asked to come down to see someone who has been brought in. Angela Strachan. Do you know anything about it?'

'No, but I'll find out for you,' Will offered, heading over towards the desk. Ginger followed, waiting as he checked the board and then turned to her with another smile. 'Seems she's Annie's patient. Cubicle three.'

'Thanks, Will.'

Ginger found Will's friend and colleague, Dr Annie Webster, talking with Cameron outside the cubicle. Her heart lurched at the sight of him, a fresh wave of desire crashing inside her. Desperate to keep things professional, she murmured a greeting before stepping inside to see Angela. Nineteen years old, with dark hair and eyes, the girl remained stubbornly silent. After a few fruitless moments alone with her, Ginger sighed and stepped back into the corridor, keeping her gaze focused on Annie. She'd always liked the young doctor and got on well with her, trusting her judgement and impressed with her level of patient care.

'What happened?' Ginger asked.

'We're not one hundred per cent sure,' Annie began, a worried frown creasing her brow. 'It seems Angela had some kind of emotional crisis. She says she wasn't trying to end things, just get away from trouble at home. There was some row with the boyfriend and she's estranged from her parents. She spent the night outside and was found wandering cold and confused in the park. I was concerned about unexplained wounds on her and called in Cameron, but when I checked her notes, I found she'd been seeing you in the past for bulimia.'

Ginger nodded. 'That's right. But she dropped out about six months ago. I've not been able to persuade her to come back.'

'Can you fill me in on the history?' Cameron asked, and Ginger battled to ignore her intense awareness of him and focus on the job at hand, handing him the summary she had printed out.

'I had no idea about any issues with self-harm but I knew things were difficult for her at home. Her parents were unsupportive and they threw her out when she hooked up with the boyfriend last year.'

Cameron sighed and ran a hand through his hair. 'Yeah, I've met them. And talked to the boyfriend. None of them seem concerned about Angela's physical or emotional state.'

'Sadly, that doesn't surprise me.' Her gaze slid to Cameron's and away again, her nerves tightening. She refocused her attention on Annie. 'I don't like to fail, but I really didn't get very far with Angela. She wasn't ready for help, refused to make any effort.'

'Well, I've suggested we admit her, at least overnight, for observation. The question is whether one or both of you can persuade Angela to see you and sort things out. Can I leave you two to discuss that? We're rushed off our feet this morning and I have other patients to see,' Annie said, apology in her blue eyes.

Ginger groaned when she found herself alone with Cameron. 'What's your assessment?' She took a few steps away, finding it hard to think when she was close to him.

'We need to try something to help Angela.' He slid his hands into his trouser pockets and Ginger swallowed, fixing her gaze on the wall behind his right shoulder, trying to ignore the way his voice made her go warm and shivery. 'Do you want me to take her on for the self-injury or refer her back to you for the bulimia?'

'If you refer her back to me it will be weeks, at best, before she'll get an appointment. We are so overloaded. Can you see her sooner?'

'Almost certainly,' he acknowledged, taking a diary out of his jacket and flicking through it, confirming he had space to fit Angela in.

She considered what was best for the girl. 'Maybe a different approach from you would help her more, anyway.'

'That's very generous of you, Ginger.'

'It's nothing of the kind,' she riposted briskly, annoyed at his amusement. 'What we think, and the conflict between us, is irrelevant when it comes to patient care.'

'I agree. But you don't know what I think.'

'Look—'

'Do you want me to tell you what I think and how I feel, Ginger?' he asked, his voice dropping to the intimate, throaty rumble that made her stomach turn over.

'No.' She jumped in alarm when he took her arm and led her down the corridor away from the busy casualty staff. 'What are you doing?'

He glanced down at her, his expression determined. 'I'm sure you'll tell me you don't have time for a coffee.'

'Of course not, I—'

'We need to talk. In private.'

She swallowed and took a deep breath, her unease increasing as he opened the door to a storage cupboard. 'We can't! Someone will see.'

'No, they won't.' He glanced both ways along the corridor, then took her hand and pulled her inside, closing the door behind them.

'I don't have time for this silliness.' Flustered, she tried without success to free her hand. 'Let me go, Cam.'

'Not until you agree to meet with me, talk with me.'

'I can't.' How could she want him so much when she knew it was wrong? She was so confused. 'We both know we're going to walk away from this in pieces, Cameron.'

'Don't.' His voice sounded raw, pained. 'Let's not put more obstacles in the way or look so far ahead.' Sliding his arms round her, he drew her close and she sucked in a breath, a tremor running through her at the feel of his body pressed against hers. She knew she should resist, but she couldn't. 'Please, Ginger. This thing between us is special, amazing. Can't we enjoy it for what it is? There's nothing we can do about the rest…not for now. Don't let it spoil what we have.'

She shook her head, her hands clenching to fists as she tried to be strong. 'I don't know.'

'Ginger—' He broke off, swearing in frustration as her pager sounded loudly in the confined space.

'Cam, I have to go.'

'I know. Damn, but the timing stinks.' He cupped her face, his head lowering to plant a heated, consuming and all-too-short kiss on her mouth. 'I'll phone you later, all right?'

She knew she should say no. But she felt pulled in two, not knowing which way to turn, scared that even when they were in opposition they couldn't keep their hands off each other. 'Let me out,' she demanded, pushing away from him.

'First promise me we'll talk tonight.'

A shiver of panic ran along her spine. Tense,

she nodded. 'All right.' Why could she never say no to this man?

Cracking open the door, he looked out. 'The coast is clear.'

Once outside, she stepped back, trying to put distance between them, but he caught her hand. 'Cameron…'

'I'll make the arrangements with Angela and ensure you're kept advised,' he promised, his sultry gaze dropping to her mouth before lifting to look deep into her eyes.

'Thanks.' She feared he could see into her soul. Every cell in her body was aroused, his gaze feeling like a physical touch. She forced her brain to function. 'I have to get back to work.'

His fingers caressed hers for a moment more before he released her. 'Later, Ginger.'

She turned and hurried away, feeling him watching her until she rounded the corner. His final words rang in her ears, feeling more like a threat than a promise.

CHAPTER TEN

As SHE prepared for bed, Ginger told herself she was relieved that Cameron's phone call had never materialised. Despite her brutal schedule and heavy workload, she had been on tenterhooks for the rest of the day, her head dreading the thought of talking with him and trying to resist his sensual persuasion, while her heart traitorously had longed to hear the sexy rumble of his voice.

She couldn't understand it. No man had ever distracted her from her work before. Yes, she had dated over the years, had enjoyed a couple of semi-serious relationships, but her work had always come first and she had never had any trouble compartmentalising her life. Cameron was different. With the complications of the Ackerman money coming between them, he was the last man she should have anything to do with.

It should be easy to say no, to stay away from him. But it wasn't. And not just because of the best sex she'd ever experienced in her life. She liked him as a man and as a doctor. She respected him. And even knowing she was laying herself open to inevitable heartache when their short but fiery time together was over, he had slipped beneath her defences and she had foolishly fallen in love with him.

Cursing her wayward heart, she left the bathroom and pulled on a pair of unsexy but wonderfully comfy pyjamas. The nights were quickly drawing in and turning cold, winds from the north letting them all know that autumn was upon them and winter would not be too far behind. Snuggling beneath the duvet, she lay back and stared at the moonlit shadows on the ceiling. What was she going to do? She—

'Oh!'

A yelp of surprise escaped as the telephone rang, sounding louder than usual in the stillness of the dark, silent bedroom. Her stomach lurched and her hand was shaking as she switched on the bedside light and reached out for the receiver.

'Hello?'

'Hi. It's me.' She needed no further identification. Cameron's husky voice sent warmth seeping through her body and set her pulse racing. 'Sorry it's late. My group meeting overran tonight. A couple of new people joined us—and someone needed a bit of time.'

'That's OK.'

'How did you get on today?'

Letting her head drop back on the pillow, she tried to still the fluttery feeling inside her. 'It was busy. By the way, I meant to thank you for what you did for Louise.'

'No problem. I liked her.' She could hear the smile in his voice. 'Is she going to keep seeing you?'

'I think so… I hope so. She says she will.'

'I'm sure you'll be good for her. I have some news for you,' he added after a short pause.

'What's that?'

'I spoke with the neurosurgeon at the specialist unit where Gary was taken. He's holding his own and has regained consciousness. He might not be going white-water rafting again for some considerable time, but his outlook is promising.'

Her breath puffed out in relief. 'That's great. Thanks for following it up. What about Angela?'

'She's staying in overnight for observation and assessment. I'll see her again tomorrow and let you know what's decided. I'm hoping I can persuade the parents and boyfriend to think of what's best for her for a change.'

'Thanks. Good luck.' Ginger didn't envy him dealing with the difficult family but had confidence he would do all he could for the troubled teenager.

Cameron was silent for a moment and when he spoke again, his voice had dropped, desire and uncertainty evident. 'Ginger, about us… What we have together is good—more than good.'

'But how can it possibly work, Cam?'

'I can't predict the future, I only know how I feel now. Do you honestly feel better with us being apart? Is it helping? Is it going to make hearing the decision any easier?'

She wanted to block out his questions, his reasoning. 'I don't know!' Gripping the phone tightly, she sucked in a ragged breath, wishing she could think straight.

'We shouldn't waste this time, Ginger. We can be together now. I want to see you, to touch you,' he murmured roughly, weakening her resolve still further.

'You said you wanted to talk.'

'That, too.' His throaty chuckle sent heat curling through her. Heat and longing. 'I do want to talk but I confess that's not the only thing on my mind.'

'Cam—'

'We have to separate our working and professional lives.'

Temptation pulled at her. 'I don't know if I can. I don't want to get hurt. I don't want to hurt you,' she confided, her throat tight.

'I'm hurting now…without you.'

So was she. That was the trouble. But she feared the pain would be even greater later on. She was already in over her head, so emotionally involved that it was going to hurt unbearably, whatever happened. Was Cameron right? For the first time in her life she loved a man. Should she just enjoy the pleasure of being with him now, even knowing it could, and likely would, all end in tears? Was she really protecting either of them by denying what they had? Even if she was never with Cameron again, she was never going to stop loving him, never going to stop wanting him, never going to forget him. The decision about the Ackerman funding was going to hurt them, no matter what the outcome, but it was out of their control.

'I need you, Ginger. Please.'

Oh, God, she had never been desired like this before, had never desired anyone so much. She loved him, and she might not have very much time with him. He was right, she should grasp what happiness she could while it was here, make the most of every stolen moment.

'Ginger?'

She swallowed, her defences in tatters, an ache of need tightening low inside her. 'How soon can you get here?' she asked, startled when the doorbell rang. 'Cam?'

'Answer the damn door!' He laughed. 'I'm freezing my rear off out here.'

Dropping the phone, she flung back the duvet and flew down the stairs, finding him standing on the doorstep, looking dark and dangerous and devilishly sexy. He stepped inside, slammed the door behind him and gathered her close. Ginger could do nothing but melt into his arms. She buried her face in his neck, feeling the coolness of his skin from the night air, breathing in the arousing male scent of him. Knowing hands slid down to cup her rear, tugging her tighter against him, leaving her in no doubt just how pleased he was to see her. He growled, bending his head to bite at the exposed skin where her neck met her shoulder. A tremor of excitement rippled down her spine. She arched against him when his fingers flexed and shaped her flesh, a whimper of need escaping as his mouth moved up her neck to her ear, licking the sensitive hollow, sucking and nibbling on her lobe.

Desperate to kiss him, to touch him, to have him naked, she wriggled out of his hold, needing to get him up to the bedroom while she still could. She gazed up into darkened grey eyes, seeing the passion, the want, knowing it matched her own. If only she could switch off all her worries and her doubts as rapidly and efficiently as Cameron switched on her urgent desire. Leading him up the stairs and into her room, she turned to push his coat off his shoulders, her fingers reaching to undo the buttons of his shirt.

'No,' he murmured, startling her as he caught her hands and stilled them.

Ginger bit her lip in confusion and disappointment. 'No?'

'Not yet.' The serious expression on his face worried her. 'I need to talk to you.'

'But—'

He raised her hands, pressing a kiss to each palm. 'I need to explain something to you—why my work is so important to me.'

'Later,' she suggested, suddenly nervous at what he would say, wanting to distract him from anything that might make things more difficult and complicated between them.

'No. Talk first.'

Anxious, she sat on the bed and watched him take his wallet from his pocket and set it on the nightstand. He removed a photograph, staring at it for several moments, unimaginable pain in his eyes, before he moved to sit beside her and hand her the picture. Ginger looked down at it, tensing, her breath trapped in her chest as she studied the face of a young dark-haired girl, aged around twelve, she estimated. The face was pretty but serious, and a secret lingered in eyes uncannily similar to Cameron's.

'Who is she?' Ginger managed, sensing the tightness in the masculine body beside her.

Cameron took the photo from her, his fingers trailing over the face. 'Molly. My daughter.'

'Right.' She struggled with the information, trying to come to terms with how much she didn't know about Cameron. Somehow she managed to keep her voice neutral. 'You're married?'

'Divorced. A long time ago.' Intent grey eyes looked into hers. 'I never would have been with you had I been committed elsewhere. I told you that in London.' Ginger nodded, acknowledging the truth of that, allowing him to continue. 'I met Lisa when I was a medical student in London. She worked behind the bar at a pub we all frequented. I fell for her, big time, and I thought she felt the same for me. We rushed into things. We were barely nineteen and married too young. I realised that quite quickly.'

When he hesitated, she squeezed his hand. 'Go on.'

'Lisa was desperate for a child. I was desperate to be a doctor. We argued about it but agreed to wait until I qualified and was more financially secure before starting a family—or so I thought.

Lisa went behind my back right away and stopped taking the Pill,' he explained with a tired sigh. 'I was annoyed, scared, but I was devoted to Molly when she was born less than a year after our marriage. What I hated was not having more time at home to be with Molly when she was young, while Lisa resented the hours I had to work.' He paused again as if steeling himself to continue. 'I soon discovered that Lisa was seeing other men. We argued, all the time, and she left me to be with someone else. I had a monumental fight to have any access to Molly at all. My daughter was everything to me, but she felt like a stranger after Lisa kept trying to keep us apart.' Ginger's fingers tightened in response to the pain of his memories.

'I should have seen what was going on, Ginger, but… It all came out later—Lisa's drinking, her boyfriend's rages. Instead of talking to me, to anyone, Molly took refuge in harming herself. She wrote it all down in a diary. A week before Molly turned twelve, her mother told her she was marrying again and they would be moving abroad, that Molly wouldn't see me much any more. Molly skipped school and was coming to find me at the hospital when she was knocked down on the road and killed.'

'Oh, my God, Cam.'

Ginger saw the tears glistening in his eyes. Aching for his loss, she scrambled to her knees behind him and wrapped her arms around him, holding him tight, understanding for the first time what drove him with such relentless determination. Her own tears spilled down her cheeks, wetting his shirt as she pressed her face to his shoulder. They were two of a kind, she realised, each doing what they could for their patients in an effort to right the wrongs of the past and for those they had lost.

For a few minutes Cameron allowed himself to lean back against Ginger and be soothed by the comfort he felt in her arms, knowing she understood and that she cared. He still found it impossibly hard to talk about Molly. He still missed her, still felt so angry, so guilty.

'Reading her diary nearly killed me. I couldn't believe Lisa hadn't noticed how unhappy Molly was. I blame myself, I should have seen something, too, even though the time we had together was limited.'

'Cameron, it wasn't your fault, any more than what happened to my sister Dee was my parents' fault.' Her hold tightened on him and he waited, wanting to believe her, part of him unable to let go of the pain. 'That's why you gave up trauma.'

It was a statement, not a question, but he nodded. 'After my disastrous time with Lisa, I was hurt, bitter. I threw myself into work, swore off marriage and relationships, of laying myself open again. When Molly died four and a half years ago, I needed to do something. As much as I loved the buzz working in A and E gave me, it was no longer enough. I needed to understand Molly and people like her. It was bad enough learning the figures for adults who injure themselves, but totally shocking to discover just how many children self-harm. And yet there weren't enough specialist services for these people. So I devoted myself to helping others as I had been unable to help Molly.'

'We're both equally driven, equally determined to set up the best facilities we can.'

'Yes.' The truth of that was obvious. He shifted, urging her round so he could look at her. Turquoise eyes swam with her tears for him, desire and despair lurking in tandem. Sighing, he cupped her face with one hand. 'Ginger, I'd never want to trample on your dreams or stop you doing what you want and need to do, but I can't stop mine, either.'

Her smile was sad. 'I know that.'

'Maybe Ackerman won't give either of us the money.'

'Maybe. But then we'll both be stuck struggling to find other funding and all our patients might suffer.' She turned her head and pressed a kiss to his palm. 'How far along are your plans?'

'A fair way. Iain Chamberlain, an old school friend and now a close neighbour, is an accountant and he's handling all the figures and financing for me. I've got some other smaller backers, plus an agreement for NHS referrals.'

'Me, too. But you sound further ahead than me.' He allowed her to remove his hand from her face, missing being able to caress her peachy-soft skin, but she didn't let go, instead linking her fingers with his. 'Have you started looking at properties or anything?'

He'd wanted to talk, but he really didn't want to get bogged down in these kinds of details, not when time with Ginger was so precious. 'Some. I've had an architect draw up some basic plans for a purpose-built clinic, but I've not finally decided whether to build from scratch or modernise existing premises. It depends on cost and what is available. You?'

'I've not had any time to look yet. It seems a bit like tempting fate. At least I have a core team of staff who are eager to come on board when—if—it goes ahead.' Worry clouded her eyes as she looked at him. 'It has to, Cam, somehow. I can't bear to think of these patients without proper care.'

'I know,' he murmured roughly.

He regretted that he had drawn her so far down this road and had made her anxious. He was the one who had said they should keep work and personal separate. Now what was he doing? Making her talk about work. Determined to distract her, he allowed one finger to trace the line of her jaw before sliding it erotically down her throat to her cleavage, teasing open her top button.

'Cam…'

Her voice had turned throaty, just as he'd hoped, and he felt a tremor quiver through her.

Leaning in, he trailed his lips across her cheek to nibble at the corner of her mouth. His finger slid another button free and explored farther, climbing the slope of one delectable full, firm breast and finding the nipple budding to his touch. He smiled at her gasp, moving back to evade her as she turned her head to seek his lips.

'Have we done talking, Ginger?' He closed his teeth on the lobe of her ear, giving it a tiny nip before sucking it into his mouth, salving with his tongue.

'Yes. Please.'

'Good.' Kicking off his shoes, he tipped her down onto the bed and worked on the rest of her buttons. 'I have other things in mind for you.'

Eyes darkening with answering desire, she smiled and echoed his own response. 'Good.'

Kneeling over her, his pulse rate sped up as her hands began undoing his shirt. He stripped it off, impatient now to see her, to touch her, to lose himself in her and forget everything else. 'Cute pyjamas,' he murmured, amused by the cartoon animals covering her from head to toe.

But she'd not be wearing them for much longer. He peeled back the edges of her top, revealing her torso to his hungry gaze. His mouth watered and his body hardened even further. Straddling her hips, he eased the material off her shoulders and partway down her back and arms, leaving her imprisoned by the fabric.

'Cameron!'

He chuckled as she struggled ineffectually to get free, taking his time to run the palm of one hand from her throat, down the steep valley between her breasts to her navel. 'You're beautiful.'

'I want to touch you, too,' she complained, still wrestling with the trapped sleeves.

'Later.' Hands firm and sure, he caressed her breasts, seeing the flush of arousal stain her silky skin, her nipples tightening as he rotated his palms over them. He wanted nothing more than to taste them, but made himself wait, teasing them both. Shifting down, he toyed with the waistband of her pyjama bottoms before stripping them down her legs, enjoying the view as he knelt between her thighs. 'Perfect.' He trailed his fingers over her feminine flesh, finding her hot and wet, her hips moving to his rhythm. 'I think I like having you captive like this. At my mercy. So I can do anything I want to you.'

A whimper of need escaped as she writhed to his touch. 'Cam, please!'

He took his time, savouring every moment as he loved her breasts with his mouth, licking, suckling, nipping, before working his way down, exploring with fingers, lips and tongue. He loved the way she responded to him, loved the soft, feminine roundness of her, the taste of her, the arousing warm summer berries scent of her skin, the noises she made. Wanting, hot, needy, he suddenly paused, trying to absorb the shocking re-alisation that had just hit him, cutting off his breath as if he had been punched in the solar plexus.

'What's wrong?' she asked, her own breath coming in ragged pants.

'Nothing.' Only that he now knew that what he had never planned on happening again, had never wanted to happen, *had* happened. He was in love with Ginger. The enormity of it, the com-plications, stilled him for a few manic heart-beats. Her amazing body squirmed beneath him, and he gazed down at her, devouring the lush and sinful curves in all the right places and the natural, firm breasts that filled his hands and drove him crazy. All of her drove him crazy. But not just her body. Not just the sex. He loved *her.* Loved everything that made her the special woman she was. Desperate not to think about what was happening to him, he freed her arms, tossing the garment aside, his fingers unsteady as he reached out to take a condom from his wallet. His voice was hoarse when he forced himself to repeat the words. 'Nothing's wrong.'

Scared, urgently needing the physical closeness, his whole body trembled as Ginger took the protection from him and tormented him as she slowly rolled it on. He leaned down, his mouth taking hers in a hot, searing, devouring kiss, letting himself drown in her sweetness, in the magic they always found together. Unable to wait any longer, he moved to her, welcoming the way she wrapped her arms and legs around him as they joined as one. He'd wanted to go slow. But he couldn't. It was too good, too immediate. They were both too needy. And they gave in to the wildness as they chased the ultimate fulfilment, flying with each other into the swirling vortex of intense pleasure.

Over the following week, Ginger had no idea what on earth she was doing. Her days were manic as she crammed in as many appointments and group counselling sessions as possible without skimping on the attention she gave each patient. On top of that she had paperwork, meetings and plans to make for her future. As for her nights... Oh, her nights! They were spent wrapped in Cameron's arms, occasionally at her rented house in town, more often at Cameron's cottage. She loved it there, the rural quiet, the cosy log fire, making love with him for hours. But she still felt she was living on borrowed time, waiting for the axe to fall, and she tried to keep part of herself back, untouched, because she very much feared she would never recover once Cameron was gone from her life.

Often she thought about his daughter, the pain of his loss, understanding so much more about him now, and why he did what he did. If only they had met under other circumstances, without the competition of the Ackerman money and what it meant to the fulfilment or ending of their dreams. Day by day it was harder to focus on the importance of her responsibilities to her patients, harder to force her personal happiness to take a back seat. But she knew time was running out.

A decision would be made and one of them would move on. Alone.

'You're amazing with those youngsters, Ginger.'

Warmed by the praise, she glanced up as Cameron came into her hospital consulting room. 'Thanks. I just want to do all I can for them.'

'You do. They're lucky to have you.' He moved close and took her hand in his. 'Thank you for letting me sit in on your group meeting this morning. I learned a lot and saw a whole different side to you. It's easy to see how you get the results you do. Your patients trust you, believe in you, and you care about them.'

'It's hard not to get emotionally involved sometimes.'

The pad of his thumb brushed back and forth across her wrist, firing her pulse. 'I know. I feel the same. Some of them are so damaged, their stories so gut-wrenching. It's like you transplant your strength into them when you give them so much of your time and your very self.'

'You do the same thing, too. And you were great with them this morning. You knew just the right things to say, caught the level on which to talk with them,' she said. Not that she was surprised, having seen him in action with his own patients. People of all ages responded to him right away.

The door opened and she snatched her hand free just in time before Pip bustled in, carrying mugs of coffee. 'I thought we could all use some before heading back to the fray,' the motherly nurse announced with a warm smile.

'Thanks, Pip.'

Taking a coffee, she sat back and sipped it, conscious of Cameron drawing up a chair beside her. Her whole body felt sensitised all the time, remembering his touch. Surely this terrible need, longing, lust—whatever it was—had to ease? But each time they were together, instead of dissipating, the urgency and specialness increased. It frightened her.

'Ginger?'

'Sorry.' She shook her head to clear her thoughts. She had tuned out and hadn't heard a word of the conversation, nor realised that Andrew, the dietitian on their team, had joined them. 'What did you say?'

Andrew opened a tin and handed it round. 'One of the parents just gave it to me as a thank-you. Why do they all bring food to a dietitian at an eating disorders clinic?'

Chuckling, Ginger smiled at him. In his early forties, he was quiet and calm, excellent at his job, swiftly building a rapport with their patients.

'I usually get chocolates,' Pip confessed. 'What are those, Andrew?'

'Home-made ginger biscuits, apparently.'

Ginger screwed up her nose. 'Not for me, thanks.'

'How can you have your name and yet hate the taste of ginger?' Andrew teased.

'I don't know.'

'What about you, Cameron?' Pip asked, drawing him into the conversation and passing him the tin.

'Thanks. I've become something of a connoisseur. The taste of Ginger is one I've come to cherish and savour.'

Ginger flushed at his outrageousness, sucking in a breath at the wicked mischief in his eyes as his gaze met hers. Fortunately his real meaning seemed to have gone over Andrew's head, if not Pip's. The nurse's eyebrows shot upwards and a shocked, delighted giggle escaped. Embarrassed,

Ginger vowed retribution. She tried to appear unmoved but her heart betrayed her by hammering in her chest, and she couldn't stop thinking about the feel of Cameron's skilful mouth all over her body.

She was relieved when Cameron's pager sounded and he glanced down at it with a frown. 'Excuse me a moment,' he murmured, crossing to the door and stepping out into the corridor where an internal hospital phone was located on the wall nearby.

'I have to get on, too.' Andrew snapped the lid back on the tin of home-made biscuits and tucked it under his arm with a grin. 'See you later.'

Rising to her feet, Ginger gathered up her files. 'Danielle Watson is being discharged today and I promised I'd look in on her and her parents before she goes. I need to set up some times to see her back in clinic.'

'How's she doing?' Pip queried with evident concern.

'She's made good progress. I wish I could do more for her, but she seems to have learned a valuable lesson from this latest scare and spell in hospital.'

'Let's hope so.' Pip paused a moment, her gaze speculative. 'Things seem to be going really well with you and Cameron. I'm so glad, lovey.'

Anxiety flared inside her. 'It doesn't mean anything. It's just a temporary thing, Pip. Neither Cameron nor I are in the market for a relationship.' She thought back to what he had said the night he had told her about Molly and his failed marriage to Lisa, the woman who had betrayed and hurt him. His certainty that he was never looking to get involved again had come through loud and clear. Fighting back her confused emotions, she tried to smile. 'If I win the Ackerman money, all my time and energy will be going into the new clinic and caring for my patients. The same for Cameron if he wins. And if he does, my time in Strathlochan will be over when the unit closes in the spring, I will be moving on.'

The words made her feel ill and she knew her performance for Pip was all bravado. Before her friend could reply, Ginger turned to go out of the door, dismayed to find Cameron leaning against the wall beside the phone. He'd been waiting for her. And he had clearly heard every word she had said to Pip. Heard, and, from the bleak expression in cold grey eyes, had been hurt. They stared at one another in silence, then Cameron stepped back.

'I have to go.'

Her throat felt tight and tears welled in her eyes as she watched him walk away from her. 'Damn, damn, damn.'

Cameron felt numb, dead inside. Ginger's words had cut him to the core. She felt nothing. To her what they had was nothing more than a temporary fling, a sexy interlude. It hurt more than he could have believed possible.

Somehow he managed to keep his mind on his work for the rest of the day, including a tricky consultation with a middle-aged woman who had been cutting herself for over twenty years. It was sad, the habit ingrained, and he knew it would be tough and take time to make a difference to her behaviour and coping methods. Thankful not to run into Ginger around the hospital, he drove home, alone, to a cold, dark cottage. Already the place felt different to him after the few nights Ginger had spent here, sharing his life, sharing his bed. But apparently sharing nothing of herself. Just sex. Tonight he couldn't be with her. He needed time away from her to think.

After a microwave meal he failed to taste, he sat staring unseeingly into the flickering flames of the fire. He wasn't sure when his feelings had changed and become so complicated. When they had first started out, he'd been so bowled over by Ginger and the chemistry they had shared that he hadn't given much thought to his emotions, to how involved he was becoming. The revelation that he loved her had shocked and scared him rigid. He'd told himself he would never trust a woman again, would never consider marriage a second time, but along had come Ginger, who was more important to him than any woman had ever been.

With Ginger he had started to think of strings and promises, of happy-ever-afters, despite the obstacles. He couldn't now imagine his life without Ginger in it. It scared the hell out of him. Because clearly her feelings were very different from his own. When the decision came through about the Ackerman funding, he and Ginger would be over. If it wasn't for his patients, his other backers, he would walk away now if it meant keeping Ginger, but he wasn't sure even that would be enough. She had made her feelings clear. Work was her life. As his had been before he had met her. She had no place in hers for anything more than a brief but pleasurable diversion. That wasn't enough for him, not any more.

With Ginger he wanted all or nothing—and he was very much afraid that for the woman he had come to love more than he had ever imagined possible, it would be nothing.

After a sleepless, lonely night, he prepared to go to the hospital, never having felt less like facing a busy day at work. A quick cup of coffee and a banana were all he could force down for breakfast, then, after checking he had everything he needed, he headed for the front door, bending down to pick up the half-dozen envelopes the postman had pushed through the letter box. He was going to set them aside to deal with when he came home, when the logo on one envelope caught his eye.

The Ackerman Corporation. Cameron felt every cell in his body freeze. Was this it? Was this the answer that would determine the course of his and Ginger's futures? He had no idea how long he stood there, just staring at it, but he finally galvanised himself into action and slit open the envelope. Drawing out the letter, he felt his pulse racing and he drew in a ragged, unsteady breath as he unfolded the page and forced himself to look at it.

It took several read-throughs before the words, and all they implied, filtered through the fog in his brain. Dread weighed heavily upon him. The decision had been made. Life would never be the same again. His insides churning, he leaned against the wall for support, absorbing the shock. The first thing he had to do was to find Ginger.

CHAPTER ELEVEN

'SARAH, please hold all my calls. And I don't want to be disturbed.'

A moment of silence greeted Ginger's request and then Sarah responded, surprise and concern evident in her voice. 'Are you all right?'

'I'm fine.' Her hand tightened its death-like grip on the receiver. 'I have some things I need to do.'

'But your appointments—'

'I've not forgotten, Sarah. I'll let you know when I'm free.'

Ginger put the phone down before her assistant could comment further. She knew she was behaving strangely but she couldn't help it. Feeling chilled to the bone, she stared at the sheet of paper that lay on her desk. Her shaking fingers cautiously moved towards it as if it were some toxic, dangerous substance she was afraid to touch. It was dangerous and she was afraid. The last thing she had expected when she had arrived at work that morning was to find the envelope embossed with the name of the Ackerman Corporation awaiting her. Decision day. She had closed herself into her office, needing to be alone to absorb the most important news of her life. Her heart had stopped as she had read the letter and she wasn't at all sure if and when it might ever begin to beat again.

She had always known that the allocation of the funding offered by the benevolent former resident of Strathlochan would mean the end of someone's dreams, an end to hope and tireless hard work undertaken to deliver the best patient care possible. Over the weeks she had tried not to think how she would feel. Nothing could have prepared her for the sense of failure and utter desolation that now held her paralysed as the news sank in that her bid had not been successful. There would be no specialist eating disorders unit in Strathlochan. She had let her patients and her staff down.

Inconsequential thoughts darted at random through her brain. How would shy, unconfident

Sarah, who had blossomed this past year, cope with finding a new job? What would her other staff do? What did the rental agreement for her house lay down about notice to quit? Come the spring, her job here would vanish and she would have to find another position elsewhere, leaving behind friends, colleagues and, most upsettingly, the patients who depended on her. She couldn't—*wouldn't*—think about Cameron. It hurt too much. She felt so numb inside that Cameron was the final straw, the death blow that finished her completely.

Voices in the outer office barely impinged on her consciousness, but she frowned when someone knocked on her door. Surely she had told Sarah she didn't want to see anyone? Against her wishes, the door opened and she glanced up, unshed tears tightening her throat and stinging her eyes as her defeated gaze clashed with Cameron's. He closed the door and leaned back against it, watching her in silence. She dimly registered that he had the twin to her own letter clutched in one hand, and that he didn't look as euphoric as she would have expected.

She felt guilty and selfish but she couldn't feel

good for Cameron, not when her patients had lost the service they so desperately needed and when all her goals were destroyed.

'Have you come here to gloat?' The words came out colder and sharper than she had intended, driven by the gut-wrenching pain and helplessness eating her away inside.

'Don't, Ginger. You know it's not like that.' She tried to close her ears to the upset in his voice, her eyes to the pain bruising his own. 'This was never a battle between us. I didn't want this to happen. It's desperately unfortunate and I'm sorry.'

'Why be sorry? You won.'

He closed the gap between them, hesitating beside her desk as she inched away from him. 'It doesn't feel that way. Ginger—'

'It's OK.'

'Damn it, no, it isn't!' His voice rose, filled with frustration and desperation. 'I never, ever wanted you to be hurt.'

'Well, you got everything else you wanted. I hope it works out for you. Now, please go.'

'Ginger—'

Her hands clenched to fists, her nails digging painfully into her palms as she battled to hold on to a fragment of her remaining composure. 'Go away, Cameron. I don't want to see or talk to you. It's finished.'

He hesitated, it seemed for an eternity. Ginger stared resolutely at her desk, willing him to leave her alone. She held her breath, the air in her office seeming thick with oppressive tension, every second ticking on the clock on her wall sounding like a gunshot. Finally, when she didn't think she could stand it another moment, Cameron made a heart-rending sound of distress and turned away, leaving her to her own misery. The closed door was symbolic of all that now placed an impenetrable barrier between them.

Ginger tried to close her mind to the memory of the terrible look on his face. He had been gutted…but no way could he feel as bad as she did. His dreams were coming true, his plans materialising, while her own had been shattered. He was moving on without her, leaving her behind, while everything she had worked so hard for was crumbling around her. The tears fell then, scorching, aching tears that ripped the heart right out of her chest. She cried as she had not done for a long, long time. Cried for her patients, her staff, her failure...cried for the loss of Cameron, the man she loved and who she would never be with again.

Cameron had never been so busy and yet the days passed with interminable slowness. The nights were even worse. Aside from his consultations and his self-help groups, he now found his time taken up with meetings and discussions with Iain, other backers and Ackerman's aides, as the push to make the new self-harm facility a reality gathered pace. But his heart wasn't in it. His chest felt tight and he was hollow inside. This was no victory. He couldn't enjoy a single second of achieving his goal, not when he knew what the decision on the funding had cost Ginger.

She had been devastated. He had seen that in her tortured expression, heard it in the strained, flat voice, and all he wanted to do was comfort her. But she wouldn't let him. That she felt she had nothing left in Strathlochan and would be moving away in a few months' time was too appalling to contemplate.

For so many years he had thought he could never feel again, yet from the moment he had met her, Ginger had turned his head, touched his heart, found his soul, helped him to heal. And yet he had never felt she was his, not completely. He hadn't wanted to believe they were on borrowed time, that she was serious when she claimed they would be over when the news of the Ackerman money came through. Now he would give anything to change reality so they could be together. But Ginger didn't want him. Whatever she had given him in bed, she had always kept something of herself apart, so sure what they had couldn't work. If only she had believed.

Every day he rang her. Every day she refused to talk to him. He should let it go. But he couldn't. He couldn't accept that they were really over, that there was no hope left. Since Molly had died, his whole focus had been on helping other people who self-harmed. He hadn't needed anyone or anything else. Now nothing mattered if he couldn't share it with Ginger. She was his soul-mate. The one person who understood what drove him, who understood his work, his patients, his life. He wanted to share all that with her but she had washed him out of her life as if he had never been, and that hurt more than anything.

'Cameron?'

Iain's voice cut through his introspection. 'Mmm?'

'What's wrong, buddy?' His friend sat opposite him, resting his arms on the table. 'You've not heard a word I said. In fact, you've not been yourself for days. I thought you'd be over the moon to win this backing and see the plans for the clinic come to fruition.'

'I am.'

'Sure, you're positively gushing with enthusiasm,' Iain drawled sarcastically.

Cameron flicked him an irritated glance. 'What did you want to talk about?'

'That can wait a few moments. Tell me what's going on.'

'Nothing. I—'

'Come on, Cameron, this is me sitting here,' Iain persisted. 'I've known you too long to take that crap.' He paused a moment, gaze intent. 'Is this something to do with that woman you were seeing? What's her name…Ginger?'

Just hearing it twisted the knife inside him. 'Yes.'

'And?'

Cameron's jaw tightened. 'Let's just say I can't

find much joy in the fulfilment of my dream when it comes at the expense of Ginger's.'

'I'm sorry.'

'Can we move on? You wanted to discuss something.' He needed to talk about anything other than Ginger.

'Properties,' his friend announced after a few moments of tense silence.

'What about them?'

'I have some more details you should look over. A couple look quite promising. Why don't we drive out and take a look this weekend?'

Unable to drum up any enthusiasm, Cameron nodded. 'Sure. Why not?'

'Great,' Iain declared with false jollity. 'By the way, the interview you recorded for the local news goes out tonight on their magazine programme. They sent a copy of the tape over. You did good.'

Running a hand through his hair, Cameron stood up. He couldn't give a fig about the TV interview and was annoyed with himself for his sour mood. This was what he had been planning for over four years. He was doing this for Molly. Whatever else happened, he couldn't forget that motivation, or the people who relied on him to make this project work.

'I have to go, I have consultations scheduled.' Thinking of Jamie, who was making good progress, should have raised his spirits, but he couldn't banish the flatness inside that had gripped him since the Ackerman letter had arrived. He slid his jacket off the back of the chair in the Chamberlains' kitchen and pulled it on. 'Give my love to Maxine and Harry.'

'Sure, buddy.' Iain rose, too, giving his shoulder a friendly slap as he walked him to the door.

Pausing a moment, Cameron wrestled with his conflicting emotions. 'We'll arrange something for Saturday and visit those properties.'

Ginger looked at the dark-haired girl who sat across from her, knowing she should feel a sense of satisfaction at how much improvement had occurred in the last weeks. She *was* pleased. Delighted. She was just finding it hard to show her emotions and her enthusiasm lately.

'You've done so well, Tess,' she praised, forcing a smile. 'You should be proud of the efforts you've made.'

Tess had put on a few kilos since first coming to them and there was more colour in her cheeks, a new spark in her eyes. It was a major break-through. What remained of concern was the girl's relationship with her parents. Ginger frowned as she looked over the latest diary entry. Since being asked to record her thoughts, Tess had written extensively, and not just about food.

'How are things at home?' she asked, watching Tess carefully.

The teenager attempted a nonchalant shrug. 'My parents are still anxious about all this, about me wanting to do something different with my life rather than what they planned for me. It's my father, mostly,' she finished with a deep sigh.

'How would you feel about attending a family session with us?'

'I don't know.'

The girl's tension was clear. Ginger paused a moment, frowning when she thought of Mr Carstairs and his gruff exterior, his rush to bury his head in the sand. The man needed to under-stand, to listen to his daughter. 'Tess, you have a right to live your life the way you want. Sometimes, discussing those things with your parents in a controlled environment can make a big difference.'

'OK, I'll think about it.'

Ginger managed another smile. 'Thank you. We'll talk about it again next week.'

After the girl had gone, Ginger folded her arms on the desk and rested her head on them. She felt exhausted, physically and mentally. The last days had taken their toll and she wasn't sure how much longer she could go on at this pace and with so little sleep. As much as she tried to avoid admitting it, to herself or anyone else, the problem was Cameron. She missed him terribly. She loved him. All of him. Yes, he was incredibly sexy and compelling, but he was also kind and compassionate, smart and funny. He made her laugh. He made her feel desired and cherished.

Now he was moving on with his life without her, as she had known would happen when the decision was made. He called her every day and left messages on her answering-machine but she couldn't talk to him. She cursed her foolishness for listening to his husky voice, for not switching off the machine and cutting off that final contact. It only made it more painful and difficult to let go. And let go she must. She had to pick herself up, start planning for the spring when she would need to move on, in every sense.

A knock on the door preceded Pip's entry into the consulting room. 'Tess Carstairs is looking well.'

'Yes.' Ginger straightened, busying herself tidying her files, avoiding Pip's penetrating gaze. 'She's worked hard.'

'Unlike you, who are working far, far *too* hard.'

'Pip—'

'Now, don't Pip me! I'm worried about you, Ginger. You can't go on like this.' Sighing, the motherly nurse sat down. 'Lovey, why are you doing this to yourself? I know it's terrible not to win the funding but there are other options and none of it means you can't see Cameron any more.'

Ginger flinched at the mention of his name. She didn't want to talk about him, think about him. She hurt so much, more than she would ever have thought possible. 'It wouldn't work, Pip.'

'So you'll just throw away the best thing that's ever happened to you?' the older woman challenged, frustration lacing her tone. 'I know he's tried to talk to you. Why won't you give him a chance?'

'There's nothing left to say.'

Shutting out her emotions, Ginger gathered her things and rose to her feet. She couldn't do this. It was always going to be a temporary thing, not only because of their work conflict but because Cameron had told her he wasn't interested in a relationship again after his unhappy marriage. What they had shared these few weeks had been amazing, special—she would never forget it, would always love him, but the complications were too many and too insurmountable, especially now he was moving on with his career and dreams while hers were stagnating, dying.

After another long day, Ginger went home to a cold, lonely house, trying to banish her disturbing thoughts by watching the local evening news. Every part of her froze in shock and pain when Cameron's face appeared on the screen. Oh, God. Her fingers shook as she reached for the remote control but they wouldn't obey her demand to turn off the television. Torturing herself, she couldn't stop looking at him, seeing the uncharacteristic pallor beneath his usually healthy complexion and the tiredness that tightened his face. As for his voice, it seemed to reach through the screen and wrap around her, throaty and intimate, his sultry grey eyes staring down the lens at her alone.

Slowly his words sank in. Apparently the local press had discovered the story of the Ackerman donation and Cameron's plans to open a specialist self-harm unit in Strathlochan. He was clear and succinct as he discussed the desperate need throughout the whole country and she was stunned when he mentioned her own field of eating disorders, too. It was bitter-sweet to know he had thought to try and help raise awareness.

Ginger was scarcely aware of the tears that were sliding down her cheeks. She leaned forward and traced the fingers of one hand down his face on the screen, the knowledge that it was really over and she would never touch him in the flesh again too much to bear.

'What the hell is this place?' Cameron groused on Sunday morning as he parked his car in an overgrown driveway of a property for sale a few miles outside Strathlochan.

He and Iain had spent all day Saturday looking at building plots, all of which were useless for a variety of reasons. He wouldn't have thought it could be so hard to find a suitable piece of land on which to build the kind of unit he needed, but it was proving to be a nightmare. As a last resort, he'd agreed to come out here with Iain today, although he held little hope it would be any use at all.

'I've lived in Strathlochan most of my life and I never even knew this was here,' Iain admitted, opening the passenger door and climbing out, the particulars and keys held in his hand. 'It says here it was a rehabilitation centre during the First and Second World Wars and since then it has been put to a variety of uses, from a children's holiday centre to a religious retreat. All sorts of things. Most recently it has belonged to a charitable trust who used it as an education centre before renting it out.'

'It doesn't look as if it's been occupied in a while,' Cameron remarked, walking towards the sprawling building, enjoying the peace and solitude of the surroundings.

'Want to see the floor plan? It's built in a U-shape with two wings leading off the central part of the facility.' He paused a moment before reading on. 'Says here that it's in good structural condition and even has a catering kitchen, along with offices, function rooms and several small dormitories.'

Cameron grunted. 'It all sounds too good to be true. Are you sure this is within budget?'

'Positive. It's been on the market for ages but the charitable trust who owns it is fussy about what use it is put to,' Iain explained. 'When I talked with the solicitor handling the sale, he said your project is just the kind of thing that would appeal to the trustees.'

They looked around the massive building. Inside it would need a lot of redecorating and re-modelling but the cost of buying it and doing all the work would be less than starting from scratch. The position was excellent, nestled within overgrown grounds and surrounded by woodland, and there was far more space than he needed. Indeed, enough space to really expand the kind of facilities he'd been planning.

For the first time since the decision had come through he felt a flicker of excitement licking inside him. If only he could share this with Ginger. The pain of losing her was far greater than any he had felt at Lisa's betrayal and the breakdown of his marriage. He simply couldn't imagine life without Ginger. If only there was some way to win her back.

'This place is amazing. It's huge!' Iain enthused when they met back in the main part of the building a short while later. 'What are you thinking?'

'Show me the floor plan again.'

Cameron spread the paper Iain gave him on a dusty old reception desk. He swore softly under his breath as the idea hit him between the eyes. 'Damn! Of course!'

'What?' Iain probed, a frown on his face.

'It's so obvious!' Cameron laughed for the first time in days. 'Why on earth didn't I think of it before?'

Puzzled, his friend shifted restlessly beside him. 'Think of what?'

'I'll tell you later.' Folding up the floor plan, Cameron turned and headed for the door. 'Come on, we have to go.'

Iain hurried after him. 'Why?'

'I'll drop you at home. There's something I have to do.'

'Talk to me, Cameron!'

'Trust me. Give me a couple of days, Iain, and I'll explain everything.'

After resisting his friend's probing questions on the journey, Cameron dropped Iain at his house before heading back towards Strathlochan. Filled with new hope, he had to find Ginger. He just hoped he wasn't too late.

Ginger stared into space, unable to concentrate on clearing the mountain of paperwork on her desk. She had come to the office on Sunday to give herself something to do, if only to stop brooding, stop thinking about—

The door to her office burst open. As if she had conjured him up from her thoughts, Cameron stood before her, looking windswept and temptingly delicious in leg-hugging jeans and a bulky jumper, his face unshaven, his grey eyes sparkling.

She opened her mouth to beg him to go away, but no sound would come out. She watched in shock as he grabbed her coat off the stand by the door and walked towards her.

'Ginger, I need you to come with me.'

'What?' Had the man taken leave of his senses? 'I can't.'

'You can,' he encouraged, taking her hand and pulling her to her feet.

'I'm not going anywhere with you! Leave me alone.'

Her good intentions failed when he helped her on with her coat, then picked up her bag and handed it to her. 'Come on.'

'Wait a minute! I—'

'Please, Ginger.'

Why could she never say no to this man? 'I don't understand,' she protested.

'You will.'

She tried to ignore the feel of her hand in his as led her from the room. He locked the door, slipped the key into her pocket, then guided her down the stairs and out of the hospital. Before she knew it, she was in his car and he was driving down the hill to the town.

'Cameron, what is going on?' she demanded, struggling with the flood of emotions washing through her at being back in his presence, the way her heart was pounding, her skin tingling, and every nerve cell aware of him.

'You'll see.'

Realising he wasn't going to divulge anything until he was ready, she lapsed into silence and turned her head to stare out of the window.

Leaving the town behind, they headed around the loch and past the sprawling grounds of Strathlochan Castle, then headed out through rolling countryside and along wooded lanes. All the traitorous part of her wanted was to devour Cameron with her gaze, touch him, kiss him. The days without him had been unbearable. She thought of him every second of the day, dreamed of him when the night brought her any sleep. Abstinence hadn't worked at all. The longing for him was worse than ever.

When they drew up in front of a substantial but neglected building in a secluded spot a few miles from Strathlochan, Ginger turned to Cameron. 'What are we doing here?'

'I'll explain when we've had a look around.' He came round and opened her door, once again taking her hand. 'Bear with me, Ginger, please.'

Cursing her weakness, unable to withdraw her hand from his, she allowed him to show her around inside the massive property. She was amazed by what she saw. It would take a lot of work to modernise it but aside from being much too big, it was just the kind of place she could envisage for her dream clinic. Pain lanced inside

280 ONE SPECIAL NIGHT...

her and she pulled away from Cameron, questioning his motives.

'Have you brought me here to rub in your victory?'

'No! Of course not.' Grey eyes darkened with hurt. 'How could you think that?'

She steeled herself against her hopeless attraction to him. She couldn't allow herself to weaken. 'Then what are we doing here?' she demanded, tossing her coat over a chair by the reception desk, before folding her arms and stepping away as he reached out to her.

If they didn't touch at all, maybe she could maintain some composure, but the instant there was any contact, that inexplicable connection and compulsion returned. She only had to think of him, look at him, to remember what it was like between them, that searing, incredible heat, the indescribable pleasure of his touch, the passion of their union.

'Did you take in what Ackerman's people said about the decision to award the money to my proposal?' Cameron asked, his words refocusing her attention.

Of course she had taken it in. Every word of the

letter ending her hopes was imprinted on her brain. Fixing him with a glare, she nodded. 'You mean about self-harm being a broader remit?'

Thrusting his hands in the pockets of his sinfully tight jeans, Cameron leaned against the reception desk. 'We've learned a lot about each other's work these last weeks and I think there are many areas where we overlap. Would you say that eating disorders were a kind of self-harm?'

'I suppose,' she agreed reluctantly. 'So what?'

'Look at this place, Ginger.' Moving, restless with suppressed energy, he spread out the floor plans.

'I have looked. I can see why you are interested in it for your clinic.' Even though it pained her to say the words.

A smile curved his sexy mouth, bringing the dimple to his cheek. 'Exactly.'

'Cameron, what is the point of this?'

'The point, my feisty love, is that we both want the same thing. We both care about our patients. We both want to set up a specialist centre to cater for their full range of needs but there is only one lot of money from Ackerman.'

'And you've won it,' she stated, unable to bear any more of this.

Cameron closed the gap between them and curled his arm around her waist. 'Think about it. We join forces, Ginger. This place is huge. A central administration and catering area, twin wings with full facilities for counselling, residential places, medical facilities, meeting rooms and space for our respective staff.' His hold tightened and he drew her against him. 'Just think what we could do with all our passion and dedication if we combined it, harnessed it. Think of all the people we could help... together.'

Ginger was thinking. She was thinking a lot of things, not least what it felt like to be held in Cameron's arms again, the length of his body against hers. All she wanted to do was melt into him and forget everything. Yet she was scared to give life to the hope and joy that threatened to bubble forth from inside her. Did she dare to believe? Could she have it all? Could she and Cameron work together, live together, love together?

'You make it sound so simple,' she managed,

her voice unsteady with all the emotion swirling inside her.

'No, it won't be simple. But it would be worth it. If you agree, I'm going to talk to Ackerman's people about it tomorrow but I'm sure they will go for it, especially as they told me the decision was very close and a hard one for Sir Morrison to make. This way he gets two for the price of one and all our patients win.'

Ginger struggled to absorb all he was saying, feeling light-headed at the sudden turnaround in her life. 'But isn't this place way outside the budget?'

'No, there's a ridiculously low price for the right buyer. It belongs to a charitable trust who are more concerned about what is done here than the amount of money they get for it.' He cupped her face in his hands, his lips brushing tantalisingly across hers, stealing her breath. 'We can do this, Ginger. Together.'

It was true they were both passionate, dedicated people, both working hard for what they believed in, driven to help those who needed them even if it cost their own happiness. Could they join forces in every sense and make both their dreams come true? Hope and belief began to close the terrible black hole of cold pain and desolation that had opened inside her since the letters had arrived.

'Cameron…'

'Please, Ginger, give this a chance. Give *us* a chance,' he cajoled, his fingers tracing her face, her neck, her throat, his magical touch making her shiver. 'I've missed you so much. I can't bear to be apart from you. For so long I closed off my emotions, told myself I didn't need anyone. But I do. I need *you*. I think we need each other. We understand each other. Share so much.' Her hands clenched in his jumper as his tongue-tip teased one corner of her mouth. 'I didn't want to be vulnerable, didn't want to risk loving again. Then I met you. What we have isn't just sex, Ginger, amazing as that is with us. I love you more than I believed it was possible to love anyone and I want to spend the rest of my life with you. Marry me, work with me. Let us be partners in every way, helping our patients, making a family of our own. Side by side, together.'

Tears trickled down her cheeks. Happy tears. Disbelieving tears. These last days she had thought she would never see Cameron again and without him she had felt more alone than at any point in her life. Now he was giving her a chance not only to realise her dreams but he was giving her the gift of his love, offering her a future that went way beyond anything she had imagined possible.

'Ginger?'

A sob escaped her and she threw herself into his arms, breathing in his earthy male scent, revelling in the feel of his strong arms closing around her and holding her tight against his body. 'I love you, too. So much.'

'We're going to make this work, Ginger.'

'Together.'

'For ever.'

Her heart swelled with love. The heat of his gaze burned her with his desire, his passion, his answering love, and Ginger slid her hand to his nape, bringing his mouth to hers. Days of deprivation overflowed in an outpouring of need. The kiss was hot, consuming, urgent, demanding. She drowned in the taste of him, unable to get close enough, her hands slipping under his jumper to explore the warm, smooth skin and rippling muscle beneath her fingers. His mouth left hers, caressing down the column of her throat, his tongue exploring the hollow where her pulse beat in frantic rhythm, the delicious rasp of his stubbled jaw exciting her, sparking a desperate ache of want.

Tangling one hand in his hair, she drew his head up, catching his lower lip between hers and sucking on it, seeing sexy grey eyes darken, feeling the shudder of need ripple through him. A need that matched her own. 'Cam, we need to go home. Now.'

'Too late.' His husky voice sent a shiver of anticipation down her spine, and he backed her up to the desk, a wicked smile curving his mouth. 'I can't wait any longer.'

'Sealing the deal?' she teased, her voice rough, her fingers fumbling with the fastening of his jeans.

'Sealing our love, our future.'

His hands worked on her own clothes and the feel of his fingers touching her bare skin made her tremble. She would never, ever get enough of this man. Happiness overwhelmed her at the knowledge that he loved her, wanted her, that they would be partners in every way. Ginger wrapped herself around him and hung on to the man who had made her dreams come true. She was never going to let him go again. Giving herself up to the magic, she met the heated demand of his body with her own, the passion of his kiss with hers, giving thanks for this incredible man and the love they shared.

Cameron was right. They understood each other, needed each other, loved each other…and they could do so much good for those who depended on them.

Together, she and Cameron could do anything.

MEDICAL™

Large Print

Titles for the next six months...

March

THE SINGLE DAD'S MARRIAGE WISH	Carol Marinelli
THE PLAYBOY DOCTOR'S PROPOSAL	Alison Roberts
THE CONSULTANT'S SURPRISE CHILD	Joanna Neil
DR FERRERO'S BABY SECRET	Jennifer Taylor
THEIR VERY SPECIAL CHILD	Dianne Drake
THE SURGEON'S RUNAWAY BRIDE	Olivia Gates

April

THE ITALIAN COUNT'S BABY	Amy Andrews
THE NURSE HE'S BEEN WAITING FOR	Meredith Webber
HIS LONG-AWAITED BRIDE	Jessica Matthews
A WOMAN TO BELONG TO	Fiona Lowe
WEDDING AT PELICAN BEACH	Emily Forbes
DR CAMPBELL'S SECRET SON	Anne Fraser

May

THE MAGIC OF CHRISTMAS	Sarah Morgan
THEIR LOST-AND-FOUND FAMILY	Marion Lennox
CHRISTMAS BRIDE-TO-BE	Alison Roberts
HIS CHRISTMAS PROPOSAL	Lucy Clark
BABY: FOUND AT CHRISTMAS	Laura Iding
THE DOCTOR'S PREGNANCY BOMBSHELL	Janice Lynn

MILLS & BOON®

Pure reading pleasure

0208 LP 2P P1 Medi